ALONE

ALSO BY CYN BALOG

Unnatural Deeds

ALONE

CYN BALOG

sourcebooks
fire

Published by Sourcebooks Fire, an imprint of Sourcebooks, Inc.
P.O. Box 4410, Naperville, Illinois 60567-4410
(630) 961-3900
Fax: (630) 961-2168
sourcebooks.com

The Library of Congress has cataloged the hardcover edition as follows:

Names: Balog, Cyn, author.
Title: Alone / Cyn Balog.
Description: Naperville, Illinois : Sourcebooks Fire, [2017] | Summary: Seda, sixteen, feels her invisible childhood nemesis, Sawyer, growing stronger just as a group of stranded teens takes shelter from a blizzard in the dilapidated mansion Seda's mother inherited.
Identifiers: LCCN 2017023033 | (alk. paper)
Subjects: | CYAC: Mansions--Fiction. | Blizzards--Fiction. | Single-parent families--Fiction. | Moving, Household--Fiction. | Horror stories.
Classification: LCC PZ7.B2138 Alo 2017 | DDC [Fic]--dc23 LC record available at https://lccn.loc.gov/2017023033

Printed and bound in the United States of America.
VP 10 9 8 7 6 5 4 3 2 1

For Muffy...

A cut above the rest

1

—

Welcome to the Bismarck-Chisholm House—
where murder is only the beginning of the fun!
Stay in one of our eighteen comfortable guest rooms.
You'll sleep like the dead. We guarantee it…

SOMETIMES I dream I am drowning.

Sometimes I dream of bloated faces, bobbing on the surface of misty waters.

And then I wake up, often screaming, heart racing, hands clenching fistfuls of my sheets.

I'm in my bed at the top of Bug House. The murky daylight casts dull prisms from my snow globes onto the attic floor. My mom started collecting those pretty winter scenes for me when I was a baby. I gaze at them, lined neatly on the shelf in front of my window. My first order of business every day is hoping they'll give me a trace of the joy they did when I was a kid.

But either they don't work that way anymore, or I don't.

Who am I kidding? It's definitely me.

I'm insane. Batshit. Nuttier than a fruitcake. Of course, that's not an official diagnosis. The official word from Dr. Batton, whose swank Copley Square office I visited only once when I was ten, was that I was bright and intelligent and a *wonderful young person*. He said it's normal for kids to have imaginary playmates.

But it gets a little sketchy when that young person grows up, and her imaginary friend decides to move in and make himself comfortable.

Not that anyone knows about that. No, these days, I'm good about keeping up appearances.

My second order of business each day is hoping that *he* won't leak into my head. That maybe I can go back to being a normal sixteen-year-old girl.

But he always comes.

He's a part of me, after all. And he's been coming more and more, invading my thoughts. *Of course I'm here, stupid.*

Sawyer. His voice in my mind is so loud that it drowns out the moaning and creaking of the walls around me.

"Seda, honey?" my mother calls cheerily. She shifts her weight on the bottom step, making the house creak more. "Up and at 'em, buckaroo!"

I force my brother's taunts away and call down the spiral

staircase, "I *am* up." My short temper is because of him, but it ends up directed at her.

She doesn't notice though. My mother has only one mood now: ecstatically happy. She says it's the air up here, which always has her taking big, deep, monster breaths as if she's trying to inhale the entire world into her lungs. But maybe it's because this is her element; after all, she made a profession out of her love for all things horror. Or maybe she really is better off without my dad, as she always claims she is.

I hear her whistling "My Darlin' Clementine" as her slippered feet happily scuffle off toward the kitchen. I put on the first clothing I find in my drawer—sweatpants and my mom's old Boston College sweatshirt—then scrape my hair into a ponytail on the top of my head as I look around the room. Mannequin body parts and other macabre props are stored up here. It's been my bedroom for only a month. I slept in the nursery with the A and Z twins when we first got here because they were afraid of ghosts and our creepy old house. But maybe they—like Mom—are getting used to this place?

The thought makes me shudder. I like my attic room because of the privacy. Plus, it's the only room that isn't ice cold, since all the heat rises up to me. But I don't like much else about this old prison of a mansion.

One of the props, Silly Sally, is sitting in the rocker by the door as I leave. She'd be perfect for the ladies' department at Macy's if it weren't for the gaping chest wound in her frilly pink blouse. "I hate you," I tell her, batting at the other mannequin body parts descending from the rafters like some odd canopy. She smiles as if the feeling is mutual. I give her a kick on the way out.

Despite the morbid stories about this place, I don't ever worry about ghosts. After all, I have Sawyer, and he is worse.

As I climb down the stairs, listening to the kids chattering in the nursery, I notice the money, accompanied by a slip of paper, on the banister's square newel post. The car keys sit atop the pile. Before I can ask, Mom calls, "I need you to go to the store for us. OK, Seda, my little kumquat?"

I blink, startled, and it's not because of the stupid nickname. I don't have a license, just a learner's permit. My mom had me driving all over the place when we first came here, but that was *back then*. Back when this was a simple two-week jaunt to get an old house she'd inherited ready for sale. There wasn't another car in sight, so she figured, why not? She's all about giving us kids *experiences*, about making sure we aren't slaves to our iPhones, like so many of my friends back home. My mother's always marching to her own drummer, general consensus be damned, usually to my horror. But back then, I had that thrilling, invincible, first-days-of-summer-vacation feeling that made anything seemed possible. Too bad that was short lived.

We've been nestled at Bug House like hermits for months. Well, that's not totally true. Mom has made weekly trips down the mountain, alone, to get the mail and a gallon of milk and make phone calls to civilization. We were supposed to go back to Boston before school started, but that time came and went, and there's no way we're getting off this mountain before the first snow.

Snow.

I peer out the window. The first dainty flakes are falling from the sky.

Snow. Oh God. Snow.

My mother appears in the doorway, her body drowning out most of the morning light from the windows behind her. She'd never be considered fat, but *substantial*, tall and striking. Mom is someone people intrinsically want to imitate. She was one of the most popular professors last year at Boston College. My father used to say all the young men in her lectures were in love with her, and all the young women wanted to be like her. She can make a glamorous entrance even when stepping out of her car to get gas. That—and her size—are what separate us, people say. I'm short and rail thin, and people don't usually pay attention to what I say or do.

"Why the sourpuss?" Mom says airily, twirling her blond curls into an elegant chignon at the base of her neck. "Is it because we're not going back just yet?"

I don't know how to respond. She says *just yet*, but I hear *ever*. The snow only cements the word in my head. My mother loves changing plans. She doesn't let other people's schedules dictate what we should do, which is why I've always missed lots of school. My mother will get these crazy ideas for adventure, like crabbing in the bay or going off to Old Sturbridge Village for a candle-making seminar, and we pick up and go. Like I said, life experience. *Books and the inside of a classroom can only teach you so much*, she says. It's part of why her students love her.

"It's only a little longer, all right?" she says, surveying the foyer in a lovestruck way. "We're very close to having a buyer for the house."

She's told me that before, but plans have changed a dozen times since June. I hate to think of what will happen if they change any more. *Fun* is what my friends used to call my mother. Except that brand of "fun" can wear you down.

"But…" I trail off, a million buts dying on my lips. But *everything*. It's one thing to live in such a remote place during the summer, when the surrounding landscape is bursting with color and the birds are singing. But in the winter?

What are you complaining about? Sawyer asks me. *People like you shouldn't be part of the general public.*

And maybe it's true. Maybe being alone with my family on the side of a mountain will keep everyone from finding out what is going on inside my head. That *he* is there, always threatening to take over. Maybe, without the outside world to intrude, Dr. Maya Helm's crazy daughter can just go on being crazy.

Not that I can tell my mother that. No, to her, Sawyer was my fictitious childhood playmate who has long been forgotten.

But the thing is, Sawyer had been coming to me more and more since we came here. He's always in the back of my head, that little voice spurring me to be a little wild whenever I want to hold back and play it safe. At first, I thought everyone had a Sawyer, like when he told me to throw a binder at Lucy Willis for calling me ugly in third grade or touch a hot radiator when I was two. Gradually though, I learned Sawyer's voice was something to keep quiet. Still, back home in Boston, I had distractions to drown him out. I had studies and color guard and friends.

Here, he is front and center in my thoughts, twenty-four seven.

And Sawyer likes it this way. Even though my head is

screaming that we need to get as far away from this place as possible, one part of me, the part of my stomach that's supposed to get queasy and unsettled, feels warm. Comfortable.

My mother comes up to me and swipes a stray lock of hair from my face. I flinch. "Don't."

"Everything's OK, love." She gives me a convincing smile, even though the world might as well be crumbling around us. "I know you're bored to death here, but I promise, we'll be back home soon."

I *wish* it was just boredom. I swallow and nod, then slide the money and keys in the pocket of my sweatshirt and head out the door before the kids can notice me. If this weather continues, I can't delay. The mountain road we live on is no joke. Our van nearly slid into a ditch during a light rain, so snow won't be any better. Not that I've ever been here in the winter.

The van creaks to life, and I pull out of the decaying three-bay garage and down the winding driveway, pinging gravel into the air behind the car. The snow looks almost pretty, landing delicately on the windshield.

It's twenty miles to Art's General, the closest store. I listen to the radio part of the way, but the only station we get is all static-filled talk about the blizzard that's coming. Twenty inches expected, at least. I switch off the radio and try to ignore the tension in my hands from gripping the steering wheel so tightly. I concentrate on the tree-lined road. Of course I'd noticed the days getting darker and colder, but I thought it was only September. I'm losing track of time now, ever since Dad checked out in the middle of the night without so much as a goodbye.

August 31. Three days before the official start of school. That was the last I saw him. The details are hazy, like a dream. Sawyer sees to that. But the outcome is the same. Dad's gone. And we are alone with Mom and her whims.

This early in the morning, the parking lot at Art's is empty. Not that it's ever crowded. When I lived in Boston, weather like this packed the stores with frantic people stocking up on bread and milk and toilet paper. But there simply *are* no people to pack Art's. It's a wonder the store stays in business, but a good thing it does. Otherwise we'd probably starve to death.

I navigate around the old snowblower carcasses he has for sale on the sidewalk, then push open the heavy door. When the bell over the door tinkles, Elmer, who took over after Art died, stares at me like I'm a ghost. "Seda?"

I give him a wave.

He cranes his neck to look out the window. "Your mom with you?"

That's the most he's said to me, ever. Elmer's never been a

talker, so if I go about my business, he should leave me alone. "Not today," I say, then turn to my list. It's a mile long and has things like hot cocoa and canned vegetables and bottled water on it.

Either she's way overestimating our appetites, or this is a *We're not going back to Boston* list.

I slump against the canned goods display, then startle at the horrifically loud crash as half a dozen tomato soup cans go scattering and rolling in all directions. Elmer just scowls and picks up his crossword puzzle. I fish after the cans and restack them quickly. As I'm piling items into a basket and trying to decide whether I should buy the kids SpaghettiOs as a treat, the bell dings again and I hear a sound that makes me freeze.

Laughter.

Art's store likely hasn't had this much noise, this much life, ever. Peeking around a tuna fish display, I watch as a group of teenagers piles inside.

They shine. They're all wearing bright, heavy coats and hats—and sunglasses, despite the lack of sun. The two girls wear meticulously applied makeup, with masses of hair heavy with styling product. The dark-haired one has devil horns on her head, and the other has her blond hair tied into ponytails with pink and blue ribbons and a giant, black heart painted on her glowing cheek. One of the boys wears a hideous mask with a long, bumpy nose, one has a hockey mask pulled up on his forehead, and another has vampire fangs. They're my age, maybe a little older, but the difference is, despite trying to look scary, they're lovely.

I can't help but stare as they start to pile gum and Twinkies and frosted doughnuts into their arms. My mom would flip if I even touched the packaging of that stuff. Elmer glares at them like they're subhuman, but do they even notice? No. They're confident. Unbreakable. Untouchable. I remember that look of invincibility from my friends back in Boston.

Boston seems a million miles and years away right now. It's hard to believe I was there only four months ago.

One of the boys—the tall, lanky one who keeps popping his fangs in and out of his mouth—scans the shelves as he saunters down the aisle toward me. He's wearing a hat that says *Panthers* and a school letter jacket that says *Wit* on the breast. I step back when his eyes focus on me.

He notices and narrows his eyes, curious at first, then amused.

I blush. I push my hair behind my ear, then look down at my Boston College sweatshirt. It has a crusted brown stain on the front. Stew, from…three nights ago? I forget.

I cross my arms in front of me and, for the first time, realize I'm not wearing a bra. I used to wear one all the time in Boston, even years before I really needed one, but they've been folded in my underwear drawer since the end of July. He comes up very, very close, smiling, and I inhale the scent of detergent, fresh and clean.

My heart is beating faster than it ever has. I'm in the process of filling my lungs with that glorious smell when he says, "Excuse me."

I am standing in front of the refrigerated case. I scuttle aside, and he reaches in and pulls out a Mountain Dew.

My mother says that's cancer in a bottle. But I'm not sure anything could kill this boy. He cocks his head at me and sidles down the aisle toward the register, where his friends are waiting.

I can't stop gawking. The guy with the bumpy-nosed mask, who's short and has one of those little GoPro cameras, has been filming the whole thing. "That your inbred trailer-trash girlfriend?" he says, smiling sadistically at me.

Mountain Dew Kid looks over his shoulder at me, then says, "She's better action than you've ever gotten, Li."

The two girls giggle as the cash register dings. The boy with the hockey mask picks a sleeve of mini doughnuts off the counter, elbows the kid with the video camera, and gives me an apologetic, *can't take these kids anywhere* look. The other members of his group are beautiful, yes, but he—with his thick mop of hair spilling out of the openings of the hockey mask and big, heavily-lidded brown eyes—is godly. He's the kind that always gets it last and worst in slasher films, just before his smart and sassy girlfriend-heroine saves the day.

When they leave, the store slides back into its tomb-like silence, and I drop the SpaghettiOs in the full cart and head to piling the items on the Pick-6 mat in front of Elmer. He rings up my purchase slowly, studying me over his bifocals as I pretend to be very interested in the Marlboros behind him. "Haven't seen your mom in a while. She OK?"

I nod. God, he does everything at slow speed. I help take cans and boxes out of the cart so I can move him along.

He nestles them, one by one, in a paper bag. "And the kids?"

I nod. "Good." I start turning the prices toward him, so he can ring faster.

"Your father?"

I cringe. I've practiced this answer, and I'm happy to say it because I know it's guaranteed to shut him up. "He left us."

As I expected, he stares at me, his grizzled jowls working, trying to come up with a diplomatic response. *I'm sorry* is what you say when someone tells you their father died, not when he doesn't want to be with you. Mom tells me he never wanted to live in the country, and that if he were still moping around, he'd spoil our fun. At least, that's what she says when she's putting on her brave face. But I know why she has me babysit the kids while she drives to Art's every week. She calls him. That's why every time she comes back, she seems a little more defeated.

On the ride home, I can't stop thinking of those kids—real, normal people my age, who live in the outside world. I have a van filled with plastic bags of food that tell me that's no longer my life. It's just me, my mother, and my siblings. Forever.

You have me.

And Sawyer. I can't forget Sawyer.

Ever.

2
—

Live—and die!—your dream.
Welcome to the most haunted mansion in Allegheny County.
Legend has it that everyone who visits succumbs to the disorienting effect of Solitude Mountain. Can you survive the night?

SAWYER chides me as I pull into our long, winding driveway, where the snow is blanketing the gravel. *Your jaw was open so wide, you could've been catching flies.*

He's right, but I couldn't help it. I'm almost sixteen. I should be planning a sweet sixteen party. But right when my life is supposed to be beginning…it's all ending. Those days of staying up all night and texting my best friends are gone. In fact, I haven't talked to Juliet or Rachel for weeks. Bug House is in a dead zone for cell phone service.

To think, my family used to be so "with it." My mom was a media arts professor with an actual social media presence and tens of thousands of followers. Her class on the modern horror film had the longest wait-list of any at the whole university. My dad was a freelance writer by day, but by night, he played the electric guitar in a band. I was officially the coolest kid in school because my mom let me stay up late to watch him play at all these trendy bars in the city. At Bug House, we don't even have a television set or a telephone. We have an old film projector and a bunch of reels of old horror movies, but my mom uses those for the book she's writing.

Before I left Boston, my friends and I used to hang out at Rachel's brownstone all the time since her parents were *never* home. The day before I left, Rachel told me that Evan Bradley, who I'd been in love with since I started kindergarten, liked me. She'd given him my number because he'd wanted to *text me over the summer*, she'd said in an excited squeal, her eyes glistening.

I knew my parents would never approve of him. He had a reputation for being a troublemaker and always having smart-ass replies in class, but I didn't care. He was dreamy, and we'd bonded in bio because he sat behind me and would crack jokes. He always told me how smart I was, so I started moving my test sheet to the corner of the desk to let him copy my answers. Being around him was a rush. So when I got the news, my best friends and I jumped up and down and hugged.

A day later, after we'd crossed the border into Pennsylvania,

I discovered the outside world couldn't quite reach this far up Solitude Mountain.

It's like my entire life got put on hold that day. I've never made out with a boy or smoked weed or done any of those foolish things that are a part of being a teenager.

And as long as I'm up here, separated from my friends and other kids, I know I never will.

Sawyer will see to that.

Bug House is really the Bismarck-Chisholm House. I don't know who Bismarck or Chisholm were, and I'm not sure anyone else does either. Their only legacy is having their names attached to this rotting monstrosity, so I'm sure they're spending their afterlife rolling in their graves.

We live in the main part of Bug House, the heart of it, the part that isn't completely falling to ruin. A few decades ago, my aunt and uncle, the former owners, bought the house and ran it as a murder mystery hotel. It was pretty groundbreaking at the time, and people would come from all over the country to stay here. Some of the most famous and glamorous people in the world visited for themed weekends. They actually paid serious cash to have the crap scared out of them. But then the idea caught on, and you didn't have to drive hours into the middle of nowhere to stay at a place like Bug House. Murder mystery events could be found on practically every street corner, so my aunt and uncle shut the place down shortly before they died.

And we're supposed to sell it. No one wants this place though. Those who do want to demolish the building. Mother refuses to sell to a buyer who'll "ruin it," which also seems to include making it a normal bed-and-breakfast or house. Though it has quaint Gothic architecture and decor, the mannequin body parts in seemingly every closet, brownish fake bloodstains on the wallpaper, and nooses hanging from ceilings aren't the kind of characteristics anyone wants to preserve. All the stuff of nightmares is housed here.

Supposedly, long ago, Bug House was a regular, stately home, but wing upon wing were added over the years. Six of them, to be exact, all stretching out in different directions in a maze of aging hallways and secret passages and history. One of the old brochures had an aerial shot of the grounds, and the mansion looks like a bug, with my big, round attic room as the head. Which is how Sawyer gave Bug House its nickname.

Despite what he tries to tell me, Sawyer isn't alive. I'd say he was dead, but I'm not sure he was ever living. My mother has a womb for twins. That's what she told me when I asked why my four younger brothers and sisters came out in pairs. I was little at the time and didn't get why I didn't have a match, and she said I did, once, but I'd absorbed him in the womb. A few days after that, I started to think that maybe the wild voice speaking inside me could be him. So I guess you could say that if he lives, he lives inside me.

When I was six or seven, I found a baby name book in my mother's dresser with two names circled: Seda and Sawyer. Seda, my name, means *Spirit of the Forest*. Sawyer, of course, is the woodcutter. Sometimes I envision him, tromping around with an ax over his shoulder. Sometimes I feel him in my gut, pushing against my stomach as if with the head of an ax, testing to find a way out.

Like I said, I don't tell people about him anymore. At first, when I told my mother about Sawyer, she laughed and said I have a *real good imagination*. But I wasn't imagining him, and eventually, Sawyer started asking me to hurt myself. Then others. It was just a suggestion, but he'd wanted me to stick a kid in fifth grade with a pair of scissors.

I managed to fight off that suggestion. And though I never told a soul about the scissors, I did tell my mom some of the other things Sawyer talked about. Thus, Dr. Batton. But when I got the distinct impression that Sawyer's intrusion in my life was supposed to be lessening with age, not growing, I decided I had to deal with him on my own. So I've let her think that

I've outgrown him. Now, when we talk about Sawyer, it's always as a joke, like he's my old imaginary friend I cast off years ago. We laugh and say, "Ha ha, remember the time Sawyer wrote all over the hallway with red crayon?" as if he was such a pleasant, quirky part of my childhood.

At least at Bug House, I never have to worry about Sawyer giving me suggestions. My siblings—Adam and Avery, who are six, and Zoe and Zain, who are just four—are my heart. Sawyer's too. I can tell by the warmth in my stomach every time I look at them. Still, my mother is wrong about me having an overactive imagination. My twin is a little…no, *a lot* of an asshole. He's bitter that I'm the one who was born. And what scares me is how much he's been with me lately. Like it's only a matter of time before he takes over.

I sneak in the back door, which leads directly to the kitchen. Shaking snowflakes from my ponytail, I stuff our purchases into the cabinets. The kids are running around the dining room table when I come in. As usual, Zoe's cries are eardrum-shattering, her energy like that of the sun. My mother is dancing about the room, setting vegetarian sausages on their plates as if she's posing for a *Better Homes & Gardens* article.

All kids think their mothers are beautiful, and I suppose I still do, despite the way this mountain has changed her. She used to be the mom who'd show up at my parents' nights at school, and every harried Boston mother would whisper, "How does she do it?" She had the most perfect arched eyebrows from meticulous plucking and wouldn't be caught dead without her tawny-colored lipstick. Now I'll walk into a room and she'll be wearing a sweater she'd packed away, which will still smell like her two-hundred-dollar-a-bottle vanilla perfume you can only buy on Newbury Street. But when she moved out here, she transitioned seamlessly into the crunchy, fresh-faced, natural mom without skipping a beat. Those harried Boston mothers would probably still be envious.

When the kids see me, they rush over, circling my waist and nearly toppling me to the ground. "Seda! Seda! Seda!" they shout like gunfire.

"Sit and finish your breakfast," I mumble affectionately, ruffling their silky locks.

Adam, Avery, Zain, and Zoe scurry to their seats. We've never cut their hair—it's a total sin to think of putting a scissor to it, as shiny and ethereal as it is. They don't like to bathe either, so they look like wild children, street urchins. They're skinny, so mostly corn-silk ringlets and knobby, bruised knees with Band-Aids. Zain crawls under the table, complaining that he hates sausage, and Zoe sings "Your Baby Has Gone Down the Plughole" to her one-eyed old doll in a voice that's never any less annoying than a whine. Avery chases her brother, and Adam stops, reads a line of his favorite novel, and shovels a forkful of eggs into his mouth every lap around the table.

I part the lace curtains and press my nose against the leaded glass, fogging it over. The lake beyond the rotting fence is so still that it's almost like on a postcard. And totally covered with snow.

"I want to play outside," Zain says from under the brocade tablecloth. Zoe bangs her doll's head on the table concussively and agrees, as usual. He could say he wants to jump from the top of a very tall building, and she'd be all in.

"You'll be sick of the snow in a week," I mumble. Turning toward the table, I take in the three links of sausage on his plate. Each has a single nibble taken out of it. I push up the tablecloth and frown at him. "And you could've saved a sausage for me."

He sticks out his pink kitten tongue.

"It's freezing out there," I tell him, grabbing a half-eaten sausage off his plate and eating it anyway. I show him my still-red fingers. "Trust me."

Adam glances up from his book, *Charlie and the Chocolate Factory*, his favorite. "He won't be able to stand the cold for a minute." He emulates someone shivering and crying at the same time. It's a very good imitation. Adam's the actor in the family.

Zoe pouts. Zain points his tongue at his brother. But Adam's right: Zain hates the cold. And this is the wrong place to be if you hate cold.

Two hundred inches.

That's how much snow Solitude Mountain got last year. I can almost imagine it burying half the house. I know this detail, because I googled it back when we lived in the outside world. I told my mother that, but she just smiled and told me we'd be back in Boston before the snow.

But it's not the snow that's bothering me. I love snow. Well, used to, when it meant ski trips and ice-skating with my friends.

Staving off a hundred little arguments and tantrums, I shovel cold eggs into my mouth and wash them down with orange juice. My mother is oblivious to it all. "Just look," she says, sitting across the table from me. "The landscape is so beautiful! The winters here must be lovely. I bet city slickers would love to come here to escape, once the estate is back in business."

Oh God. My mother actually still believes someone will want to buy this place and run it like her aunt and uncle did. She mentions potential buyers all the time, but the deals always fall through. A couple of times, she even mentioned moving up here full-time and running the murder mystery mansion herself. As I look around the room, I cringe. My mother's aunt and uncle must have been really macabre, because the dining room resembles the Haunted Mansion at Disney World, with heavy velvet drapes, giant wrought iron candlesticks, and ornate, high-backed chairs. All we need are gossamer forms in evening dress waltzing around us to complete the picture. I can't see people coming here to escape. This is a place to escape *from*. "Mom. No. We're here because no one else wants to stay in this hellhole."

"Oh, you are such a negative Nelly." She smiles brightly, wadding up a napkin and tossing it right at my face. "Well, of course not *now*. A little elbow grease is all the place needs."

"All the elbow grease in the world couldn't save this house, but whatever," I grumble.

She opens her mouth to reply, but nothing comes out. Instead, she rolls her eyes as if I've told an amusing and slightly inappropriate joke. She thinks I've been a spoiled, disengaged teenager because I lost my iPhone.

She is so wrong.

Zain stares at me pitifully, bottom lip stuck out. I look past the fogged windowpanes toward the backyard and wipe my mouth with my napkin. "I'll take him out for a few minutes. He'll only pester us all day if I don't," I say lightly, standing up from the table as Zain whoops with glee and runs to get his Buzz Lightyear jacket. "And that whining will drive us insane."

My mother smiles. "Thank you. I will be upstairs writing. Oh!" She rubs her hands together. "Someone has a surprise under his or her plate. Whoever gets it is queen or king for the day and doesn't have to help with chores."

My mother's always doing stuff like this—playing games, surprising us to shake up the routine. Not that I need any more surprises, what with the fake dead rat and brains in a jar we found during our cleaning this week. I halfheartedly reach for my plate when my mother gives me a hopeful look. She has to know the amusements that excite my siblings just don't do it for me anymore. The kids eagerly shove aside their plates, and Zoe squeals when she's the winner. The others pretend-pout, but the excitement of playing one of Mom's games is enough to keep them all happy. Young kids are easy to entertain. That's why they don't mind living here. Maybe if I'd been moved here when I was six, I wouldn't mind it either.

Getting four little kids ready to brave the snow is like trying to herd cats. We stand in the enormous, drafty foyer and tear at the coatrack until it's bare. There are mismatched gloves and scarves, boots that don't fit so well anymore, and a flurry of cries of "Button this!" or "Zip that!" until we're all ready. As usual, getting them bundled to brave the elements means I forget something for myself. Luckily, Adam was born an old soul. He hands me my hat, and I tuck my ponytail into it. "Thank you, my dear." I grin at him. He pretends to be shot in the heart and falls down dead on the welcome mat.

Once we're all uniformed, my mother pulls me into a hug. She kisses the top of my head. "Ah, Seda," she whispers into my ear. "You're such a good mother hen. What would I ever do without my mini-me?"

Mini-me. She calls me that all the time, and maybe it used to be true. But she's always smiling, and I'm always…well…not. I'm struck by a momentary feeling of guilt. "I'm sorry, Mom."

She shakes her head. "I know all you've given up. I promise you, I will make it up to you with something really fun."

Lately, her idea of fun has been making ornaments out of acorns. Sewing aprons for us to use when we help her in the kitchen. Finger painting with mud from the overgrown garden out back. All perfectly fine activities for your average six-year-old, but Juliet, Rachel, and Evan wouldn't be caught dead doing such things. She lives to make the twins happy, and sometimes I get left out. I try to muster a smile, but it doesn't come.

Adam wraps *Charlie and the Chocolate Factory* under his scarf and tugs me out the door. We brave our way down the icy stone steps, then tromp across the first new powder of the season. The lawn's steep slope makes what my mother keeps saying will probably be a good sledding hill. When I point out that we don't have sleds, my mother claims we can use anything. She and my dad used to go sledding on pizza boxes when they were in college. Not like we even have those.

Adam sits down on a rusting wrought iron chair on the patio and starts to read his book, oblivious to the tiny flakes landing on the pages. Zoe and Zain rush forward, tongues wagging back and forth like pendulums to catch snowflakes. "I'm queen, I'm queen! Bow to me, loyal subjects!" Zoe cries, though no one does. Avery kicks a stone across the lawn like it's a soccer ball. The sky's an ugly steel gray.

We live near the top of Solitude Mountain, the sole rulers and inhabitants of this kingdom, as there are no other houses or signs of life to be seen in any direction. Birds and other animals have the sense to stay away too. Everything is so still, so quiet that it's hard to believe there's life beyond these borders.

I should run away before they find out what I really am, before I lose control of Sawyer.

Good luck with that. Little Seda, afraid of her own shadow, Sawyer's bitter voice responds. As long as we're here, he'll never let me forget that I'm the one who won our mother's womb.

"I would. I *could*," I insist, but my voice is less than a murmur.

He's right though. This place is like a snow globe, trapping me inside. And I am drowning here.

No one else wants to stay in this hellhole, I'd said.

Sawyer's laughter buffets my eardrums. *Yet, lucky us. Here we are.*

MEET YOUR INNKEEPERS,
ELLIE AND EDWARD FRICK

Ellie and Edward Frick have been owners and innkeepers of Bismarck-Chisholm House since 1983. Both actors by trade with a shared love of everything macabre, they appeared in many off-Broadway productions, including many murder mystery theater productions, such as *There's a Snake in My Boot* (a Wild West murder) and *Here Dies the Bride* (a wedding murder). They spent many vacations hiking the Allegheny Mountains and fell in love with the beauty of western Pennsylvania. When they stumbled upon the Bismarck-Chisholm House during a long hike up Solitude Mountain, an idea was born. The inn was purchased in late 1983 and opened in 1985 after extensive renovations.

Give them a call today! Ellie and Edward are always happy to meet new victims. They're dying to have you!

ONCE the kids are settled down for their naps, I tiptoe down the hallway, rubbing the chill from my arms and wondering for the thousandth time if my mother will ever succeed in selling this place.

Impossible.

I never knew my great-aunt and great-uncle, but it's clear they worked hard to make Bug House scary. They bricked in the bow picture windows to give the rooms a dark, claustrophobic feeling. They outfitted the house with the dreariest, most macabre furnishings. They even put little brass placards above some of the guest bedroom doors with ghastly information about the people who'd supposedly lived there at one time or another. I remember looking at the faded brass plaques the day we got here and thinking I'd never be able to spend one night in this house of horrors, much less two weeks.

Back then, I'd been nervous, creeped out, but mostly… excited. After all, this was our vacation. *Our latest adventure,* my mom kept calling it. She'd told us we could stay in a hotel in Erie, which is forty miles away, while we checked the place out. That's where her aunt and uncle's lawyer lived. She figured she could arrange to meet with the people who would clean out the house and talk to a potential buyer, who wanted to demolish the whole place and put up a ski resort. She told me that once we sold the house, we'd have lots and lots of money. We'd be able to go on a *real* vacation next year, maybe even a cruise to the Caribbean.

We spent three nights in that hotel, the Sunscape Villas,

right there on Lake Erie. The first day, we went boating on the lake. The next day, we were supposed to go up to the house to poke around and then drive to a water park.

We never made it to the water park. The change was quicker than flipping on a light switch. Mom saw Bug House, and every one of those plans for the future fell away.

Two days later, she moved us into the house. Three days after that, she called the real estate agent and told her that she'd only sell the property to someone who'd run it the way her aunt and uncle had.

She'd never even consulted with my dad. That was probably the first nail in the coffin that was their marriage. The few days he was here, my dad yelled all the time and stomped just about everywhere, his face permanently twisted in distaste. *Maya, you're insane*, I heard him mutter more than once. *You'll be here forever, trying to sell this place. No one will buy it in this condition, and I don't want my kids growing up in a house of horrors.*

In most of Bug House, it's almost as frigid inside as out. That's because of the damned southeastern-most wing, the burned-out wing. My mother covered the entrance to it in heavy-duty plastic to keep out the elements, but the duct tape holding up the barrier is now separating from the wall. I blow hot air into my hands, stand on the window ledge, and flatten the tarp against the charred wood. The tape immediately springs up again, and an icy blast stings my cheeks, which are already raw from this morning.

The Mulberry Room—my mother's office—down the hall is just that: bundles of purple berries hanging in tattered wallpaper. Her desk is empty except for a small CD player–radio playing Rachmaninoff, though my mother is nowhere to be seen. I'm standing there in the hallway, looking at the faded brass placard and wondering where she is, when the long shadows start to creep in. The way this house is situated, this wing gets brilliant sun in the morning but grows darker and creepier after the clock strikes noon.

The Mulberry Room belonged to Delores Hall in the 1700s. She was found hanging from the balcony railing of this room, said to be distraught over unrequited love.

The Mulberry Room is across from my mom's bedroom, which is yellow in a sickly, mustardy way. There's no plaque there. Next to the door is a bright rectangle of striped wallpaper with scratches along the edge where someone must have pried the plaque off. Sometimes I imagine what her plaque would say. *This room belonged to Maya Helm, who dragged her children out to the middle of nowhere and never returned.*

The braided oval rug that had been there before is gone now, leaving a ghostly outline on the floor where the wood finish had been protected from wear. My mother has a book somewhere, filled with things she wanted to do to get this house ready to sell, and "clean rugs" is probably number 4,786 on the agenda.

The house creaks again, settling a little more under the weight of each new snowflake. The angles where the ceiling meets the wall are awkward and bulging. It's likely from more water damage because the ceramic shingles on the roof look about a hundred years old and are mostly broken, but I won't tell my mother that. She has enough to worry about.

I walk down the hall a way, pausing to reread the plaques as I go. The thing about these plaques is that they never say anything good about a person's life. Only that they lived here and how they died. Likely, these placards aren't even true. I can imagine my crazy old aunt and uncle coming up with all these grisly stories to entertain guests. I think they must have been quite the characters.

My mother told me the plaques are, and I quote, "derivative drivel." She never reads anything that's written and likes it. Mostly, she just sees how she can improve it. She says all writers are like that, and fiction writers are worst of all. She says writers sometimes get so caught up in their stories that reality escapes them. I believe that because sometimes she is so in her head, thinking up a story, that she doesn't realize we kids are there.

Anyway, that's why those stories don't scare me. The truth? That's different.

I hear a sound inside the Strawberry Room, so I reverse direction and peek inside. The Strawberry Room is not nearly as sweet as it sounds, and it's hard to believe it ever had anything to do with its namesake. Despite the cheerful pink color of its wallpaper, it's hopelessly narrow and windowless. I can stand in the center and touch the walls on either side of me. I think it may have been part of the Mulberry Room, but a wall was constructed long ago, separating the two. It's a place you put things you want to forget. Considering its occupant, Esther Wise, was a famous actress who burned to death, maybe where the inn's owners put *people* they wanted to forget too. I shudder as I peer inside and see the bed on the far wall. It's a twin bed, and it takes up the entire space. One has to climb over the footboard and crawl up to get under the covers. But there's only a stained mattress now.

The room is otherwise empty.

"Mom?" My voice echoes through the arched hallway, and without a touch, I get the sense someone is nearby.

Breathing. A diseased rasping for air.

Sawyer is laughing in my ears. *Aw, wittle baby Seda is scared again.*

I whirl around and squint down the hall. I see the dark, shapeless outline of something lumbering away from me, then dragging itself into the shadows beyond the arched doorway that leads to the main house. For a moment, it stands at the top of the staircase, teetering there, as if deciding whether to topple over.

And then it disappears from sight down into the stairwell, without a sound.

"Mom?" I call again, daring myself to hope that was her. But I know the light sweep of her feet upon the floor. The blood inside my veins has chilled; my voice is quieter than a sigh. My stomach roils.

It's him.

The floorboards behind me creak, and a voice says, "Hmm?"

I jump to the sky. My mother is standing outside the Blue Room, holding a dusty film reel. *The Blue Room belonged to playwright Edgar Wise. He choked to death in 1910 on a bottle cap for his eye drops.*

"Do you want to watch this movie with me?" Mom asks.

Her mind is like one of the quarter dispensers outside Art's General Store and Hardware that spit out little toys in plastic eggs. I never know what'll come out of it, but it's never as good as what I'm hoping for. Her thoughts are always so scattered when she's working on her writing that I never know what to expect.

"OK, I guess."

I don't like horror movies. Not that they creep me out; in fact, it's the opposite. I've seen thousands of them, and my mother has talked them down to such a science that they're all pretty dull. I can't stand watching them with her because she always switches off the projector during an intense scene so that she can scribble some notes. But it's still nice to spend one-on-one time with her.

We sit down on the sofa in the Blue Room, in front of the screen, and she starts the projector. *Dawn of the Dead*. Fantastic. At least it isn't the remake. The original film I can stomach.

She picks up her pad and pen and scribbles. "That would be an interesting idea for the house. Have everyone stuck inside, while zombies try to invade."

I throw myself against the back of the sofa. "Mom. Zombies are so overdone. No one cares about suspense and buildup. If you want to freak out people today, a movie has to be really in-your-face gory and gross. Like *Saw. Final Destination.* Everything else is boring to them."

My mother shrugs. "Well, say what you want. I think if

the right person takes over the property, with the right advertising, the right investment, and the right story lines, this place can do phenomenally."

I sigh. *And the right amount of insanity.*

"I was thinking," she says dreamily as the opening credits roll. "It's a big day tomorrow. We should do something together. A game maybe. For fun. Like a scavenger hunt?"

I'm not really listening. I'm still thinking about the shadow I saw down the hallway.

"You know, just for a change. I can break you into two teams and leave clues everywhere. Wouldn't that be fun? There are so many rooms in this house and only so many times the kids can play hide-and-seek. I'd hate for us to all go mad, doing the same things, over and over again, right?"

"Right," I agree, still only half listening.

"So…tomorrow? Scavenger hunt?"

The words hit me suddenly. *Scavenger hunt.* My mom's always playing games, doing things to shake up the days and make the kids happy, which is why they're usually stuck to her like glue. "Sounds good, Mom. I should probably go check on the kids though." I swallow. "I-I thought I saw something."

Mom's voice is faraway, like it always is whenever she's spinning a new idea in her head. "What did you see?"

Wittle Seda, you're, like, three steps from the lunatic asylum.
I push my hand against my abdomen. "Nothing. I mean, I
thought I heard Zo crying."

Not waiting for a response, I dash down the hallway to
the main house. Beyond the long, narrow hallway that leads
to the rotting spiral stairs up to my haven is a room with white
double doors, both of which are shut. It's the nursery, and the
sweetest room in the place, though that's not saying much. It
catches the bright sun of morning and is papered with cheerful pink roses on trellises. All the furniture is white wicker, and
there are pictures of Bambi and Thumper on the walls. The
throw rugs are shaped like giant ladybugs, and about a thousand stuffed animals and dolls line the shelves. Many were
dusty and just plain freaky looking, but my mother cleaned
them up and made them good as new. Each one of them has
a marking on its foot or a tag: *Forever.* I liked that about them
when we arrived, because back then, forever wasn't such a
bad thing.

There isn't a sound coming from the room as I pull open
the heavy door. All the kids are heavy sleepers who've been
known to nap until dinnertime. I guess this place has a way of
exhausting people, because all the rooms are so very far apart.
Zoe is lying in her fluffy white bed, looking like an angel. Golly,

her old one-eyed doll, stares up at me with an endless wink. The other kids are sleeping soundly too.

I turn to leave, and that's when I feel a damp sensation under my feet. The floorboards are wet.

"Did you hear him too?" Zoe whispers. I turn. She's now wide awake.

"Was that you, out of your room, just now?" I ask, knowing it wasn't. It couldn't be. She's in the same spot she was when I tucked her in an hour ago. And she's too small to make a dark figure like that.

"He was out front," she says, motioning to the window with her chin.

"Who?"

She shrugs.

I walk to the window and tilt the blinds. This room has a view of the front stoop, with its crumbling brick steps and giant urns on either side, which have only held tangles of weeds. A blanket of snow has covered all that imperfection though. I start to tell her she's only dreamed it, when I see something that makes me stop.

There are footprints in the snow.

Ours, I think.

Sawyer snorts. *You played in the back of the house, dummy.*

And as usual, he's right. We'd raced to the pond, to the tree line, and then we'd come back, out of breath and red-cheeked, snowflakes in our hair. We'd tried to make a snowman but only got the head formed. The snow had been too powdery, and the air was too frigid.

No. Those prints had to be Adam's. He must have slipped out front. For a six-year-old, he's shaping up to be big and husky, like his dad. Or…

Dad. Maybe it's Dad.

I catch myself before I can dare to think that what happened all those months ago was only in my mind. Maybe he's been lonely in Boston, hoping for us to come back.

"I bet he tried to ring the doorbell," Zoe murmurs, turning over, her voice heavy again with sleep.

"He who?" I ask, peering out the window into the dull grayness. The doorbell has never worked, because the wiring in this house is a mess. Whenever I flip a switch, I consider it a small miracle that it actually does what it's intended to do. More items on my mother's list.

Zoe's voice is barely a breath. "I don't know. Someone. He's inside now."

4

Your stay at Bismarck-Chisholm will leave
you feeling relaxed and refreshed…not!

This is *not* your ordinary vacation. Located in one
of the most isolated parts of the Northeast, the
Bismarck-Chisholm House is unique. There is something beautiful—but very eerie—about this property
on lonely Solitude Mountain. Some guests remark
that they can feel an odd presence, as if someone is
following them or watching their every move. Ghosts?
Perhaps. If you feel the need to leave in the middle of
the night, you won't be the first. If you want to sleep
with one eye open, it's probably for the best. Are you
brave enough to stay with us?

INSIDE. He's inside.

Unless by "he" Zoe means one of the many sparrows or
squirrels that seem to find their way into our chimneys—or
are simply part of Zoe's make-believe world—there's only one
person it can be.

Dad.

We are too far away from everything and everyone at Bug House. No other soul has any reason or the lack of sense to come up here.

The thought makes me shudder with an odd combination of fear and hope.

Zoe hadn't answered me when I asked the inevitable *who*. She'd simply rolled over and gone back to her nap. As much as I love my siblings, sometimes I don't. They love horror movies— the gorier the better—so they know how to scare people. They probably know this house better than Mom and I put together, because they're constantly slipping in and out of the rooms while playing hide-and-seek. Often I'll be reading by candle-light, and one will simply appear at the foot of my bed without having made a single noise on the staircase. Or Zoe will pop her head out of the hamper when I go to retrieve the laundry. Avery's a little sadistic and likes to play games with the bloody props we find all over the house. Yesterday, she left a bloody eyeball in my water glass.

So sometimes, alone is better.

When Zoe drifted back to sleep, clutching Golly, I got on my hands and knees and ran a finger over the wet spots on the dusty floor. Then I panned the room for evidence that some watery ghost had been leaving wet footsteps in the nursery, only to discover a glass of water on Adam's bedside table. He has a habit of filling glasses until they are impossibly full, so they spill when he carries them. Adam isn't always the most sure-footed of kids, and as he's been growing, he's constantly tripping over his big, clown feet.

I walk back to the main part of the house, my skin skittering with shivers. Things are always a little off in Bug House, but now, something feels even more so. Someone is here. I can feel the presence. Wind rustles through plastic. I peer over the mahogany railing at the entrance to the burned-out wing. The tape hasn't held, leaving a gaping hole, and the curtain is billowing wildly in the air as dried leaves scatter across the parquet floor.

Dad. I lay my hand on the railing and guide myself down the worn stair treads. But I only make it the first two steps before I see them, reflecting the small bit of daylight that has managed to find its way into the home. Bits of dirty slush and pine needles from the outside, trailing across the floor.

Footprints.

Real, human footprints. This time, there's no mistake.

"Say-say," my mother's voice calls. "Where are you, sweetness?"

I jump. My voice shakes. "What?"

I'm still looking at the watery trail when she says the

dreaded words. "I forgot to take out the stew meat for dinner. Could you?"

I say nothing, but the wind whistles in through the open flaps of plastic, making enough noise for both of us.

I follow the trail with my eyes. It lightens toward the center of the foyer, but the last traces of earth and pine point toward the kitchen. I take a breath. Then I cross the foyer and push the kitchen door open with grim determination.

It's the same as it's ever been. White porcelain tiles with blue pastoral scenes. A pan, coated in scrambled egg bits, is soaking in the sink, collecting the tinny drips from that faucet. Every faucet in this house drips in a maniacal, Chinese-water-torture way.

Clean plates are stacked in the dish tray, and beside that sits a wood block filled with knives. It's not new, but it's not like the crumbling rest of the house. When my aunt and uncle ran the place, they sank most of their renovation budget into this kitchen. There are a giant butcher block island and a massive industrial stove with two ovens. That's overkill for the six of us, but "it would sure come in handy if we made this into a working bed-and-breakfast," my mother had said, which had made me shiver. It was the first indication she was toying with the idea of keeping this place.

"Dad?" I call, shattering the silence.

My eyes trail to the white floor. It's perfectly clean. Not a dirty, wet footprint in sight.

I exhale the breath I'd been holding, but suck it in again when I see the door to the freezer.

When I first peeked, I was amazed to see the sheer volume of space in there. Although empty, it could easily hold half of Art's General. Mom said this house needed a massive freezer to hold enough food so there was no chance of any guests starving to death while snowbound during an unexpected winter storm. Back when Bug House was a place we were selling, that meant nothing.

Now it's all I can think of.

I pry the lid off the stout tea canister on the counter. The key is pillowed between tea bags that smell faintly of Sleepytime spices.

Despite every muscle in my body urging me not to, I push the key into the lock and twist. Then I pull up the freezer's handle and hear the pop of the suction releasing as the insulated door opens. A puff of white frost billows out to greet me as I pull the heavy door toward me and peer into the darkness at the silent, hulking shapes that could be any of a million things. The chain for the light is all the way in the center of the room. Dumb, dumb idea, renovators.

Get it, get out.

As heavy as the door is, I would sacrifice a limb before I let it force its way closed on me. Even my mother never goes further than a few steps, because if that door closes, and nobody knows you're in there, banging with all your might won't do any good. The door is just too thick. No one will hear. There are scrapes up and down the inside of the door, brown with what looks like old blood. I know my aunt and uncle did that to scare people, but still…

Thankfully, the stew meat is at the very front of the freezer. I can reach most of what we need on the metal shelving while still standing in the doorway to keep the door from closing. I reach out to the shelf and root around, groping for a package that feels the right size. I keep pulling them into the light, then tossing them back. Pork shoulder…ribs…filet…Hunter Hot Dogs, the package with the dancing hot dog … Shit. Where the…? Chuck for stew. *Yes!*

I smile at my victory, then shove the heavy door shut, fasten the lock, and turn.

A man is standing in the kitchen doorway, an ax propped on one shoulder.

5

Our twenty-three acres are located at the very top of Solitude Mountain, deep within the heart of the Alleghenies. Skiing is plentiful on Funnel Mountain, a short forty-five-minute drive away. But other than that? Nothing. Nothing for miles and miles. So don't worry. No one will hear your screams.

I SURPRISE myself by not jumping or crying out. The face is wide-eyed and white, but not ghostly, not menacing. Simply curious. Young…he's young. Older than me, definitely, but still teetering on the brink of manhood. Definitely handsome, like an actor out of a movie.

"Sawyer?" My voice trembles.

But even as I say the name, I know he's not my brother. Sawyer's inside me, so I know him like I know myself. Plus, the ax is shaking—trembling—in the boy's hands. He's holding it out in front of him like he isn't used to such a weapon and has no idea how to use it. In my mind, Sawyer lifts an ax like it's another limb. And there's no trace of Sawyer's mischievous smirk.

"Who are you?" he asks me, his voice echoing against the porcelain tile, and at the same time I see the hockey mask pushed up onto his forehead and recognize who he is. He's wearing a tight skullcap now, studded with melting snowflakes, but everything else is as I remember it, even those arresting brown eyes. He's one of the boys from Art's.

"Who are *you*?" I fire back. "I live here."

He lowers the ax, a bewildered expression on his face. "I thought no one lived here."

I know I'm blushing, even if our new guest isn't all that bright. My social muscles are entirely too rusty from disuse. Didn't he see our footprints in the snow outside? The pile of wet clothes we'd left in the foyer? The old Dodge Caravan in the garage? Obviously *someone* lives here.

He looks around the cobwebbed corners of the ceiling, which do have a way of making our house look uninhabited. The more I take him in, the more I realize that I thought he was a man because of his extra padding. He's wearing a red ski jacket, which helps him to take up much of the empty space in the doorway. His cheeks are as red as the jacket though, almost painfully windburned, and he has a bloody gash over one eye that I'm sure I would've noticed while we were in the store.

"We?" he repeats.

"Me and my brothers and sisters. And my mother."

"Who is Sawyer?" he asks.

"He's…no one." I cross my arms in front of myself, shivering. "Why are you here? In our home?"

His eyes widen. He peels the wool hat off his head, revealing that unruly mop of cinnamon-colored static cling. "Well, you didn't answer when I rang the doorbell. And I, uh…I don't really know. We came up from Pittsburgh. Shady View Academy. We were on our way to Funnel Mountain. And that storm came up pretty fast. We slid off the road and got stuck in a snowdrift, you know?" He shrugs. Is he asking me?

"What is Funnel Mountain?" I ask stupidly.

"Ski resort?" He lets out a nervous laugh, like he can't believe he's here having this conversation with me. "You've been here how long? Uh. Yeah, your driveway was the last one we passed. We saw the house from the road down below. So we climbed up and…yeah. This place is wicked."

"You *climbed up* here?"

"Well, not exactly. We hiked up the road."

Carver Hill Road is what he's talking about. It's so steep that you might as well be climbing. Our Dodge Caravan growls like a mad bitch during the ascent. "Who are *we*?"

"Me and a few of my friends."

His friends. I can't believe it. His friends, his glorious, beautiful, full-of-life friends are here? On my mountain? "Friends?"

"Like I said. We got stuck and…" He reaches into his pocket and pulls out something I haven't seen since we tucked ours in the drawers of our night tables. A cell phone. "No reception."

Well, duh. "This is a dead zone."

He raises an eyebrow. "Really? On top of a mountain?"

I nod. "We don't have a phone either."

"You don't have a landline?" he repeats, looking around like he's going to prove me wrong and pull one out of the sink. "Like, how? What happened to this place?"

"Nothing. I mean, it's falling apart, obviously," I chatter nervously. I set the stew meat on the counter to thaw. "It used to be a murder mystery hotel."

He laughs for the first time, a deep, rich sound, so full of life. As much as I know he should keep it down, I love the way the sound wraps around my eardrums. "I think it still is."

"I don't understand," I say, to which he looks at me like I have something coming out of my nose. Maybe I do. I rub it—it's dry, no drip—and blush even more. I am so stupid. "Uh. What's your name?"

"Oh. Sorry." He sets the ax down on the butcher block counter, peels off a heavy glove, and offers his hand to me. "Heath Hunter."

Heath Hunter. It's a strong name, a good name, a name that only an important person, a person with a place in the outside world, could carry.

I stare at Heath Hunter's hand. Nobody's offered me a hand to shake—ever. But I can do this. I lean forward, touching the tips of my icy fingers lightly against his warm, pleasant ones. And I shake, trying to match his smile.

My eyes drift over to the ax on the counter. The handle is worn and splintering, and the blade is coated in dried blood and long strands of dark hair.

6

—

Our eighteen well-appointed, themed guest rooms will make you comfortable with fluffy towels, quality linens, and pillow-top mattresses—but not too comfortable! Help yourself to the freshly baked homemade cookies from the cookie jar, and enjoy our full selection of hot and cold beverages, available twenty-four seven in the lobby, if you can make it there alive.

MY new guest follows my gaze to the bloody ax.

"It's um…a prop. I thought you were a wild animal. I was going to pop you over the head. Not really though, obviously," he explains quickly, touching the blade. "See? Plastic."

"Prop?"

"Yeah. You know. I'm Jason." He pulls the hockey mask down and fixes it over his face for a beat, then pushes it back up.

I raise an eyebrow. "Why?"

He lets out a snort of a laugh. "For Halloween?" I'm staring at him, thinking he must be mistaken—Halloween is weeks away—when he says, "Haven't you ever seen *Friday the Thirteenth*?"

Friday the Thirteenth and all its many sequels. In fact, I don't think there's a horror movie I *haven't* seen. It goes with the territory of being my mother's daughter. "You mean Halloween is *today*?"

He looks a bit flustered, and I know that's all my doing, though I can't be sure what I've done. When I lived in Boston, I could talk all day with Evan Bradley and not even blush. Now, tomatoes have nothing on me. I knew carrying on a normal conversation with someone my age would be hard after all these months, but I didn't realize I was this out of it. It's like we're not even speaking the same language. "Yeah. People ski in costumes at the resort," he says.

Shit. My siblings are going to freak out. I always took them trick-or-treating around our apartment complex in Boston. I'd assumed we'd be back there before Halloween rolled around again. But if Halloween is tonight, that means my birthday is only two days away. Rachel used to say that I came around on the ass-end of Halloween. We used to talk about how awesome it would be to have a Halloween-themed Sweet Sixteen bash. I swallow the sour taste in my throat. "Oh. Of course."

He's on to me. I've probably already done a thousand things

to show him how weird I am, judging by the way he's studying me cautiously. If I hope to have any further conversation with him, I have to stop saying so much.

Even so, it's thrilling. I can't remember the last time my heart raced so quickly for a good reason.

He snaps his fingers. "OK, you got two names to call me, and I haven't gotten even one for you. Hardly seems fair."

"Seda Helm," I say softly.

"Seda? That's nice. It's nice to meet you."

"You can call me Say. Some people do." Though not many anymore.

He smiles in a way that drives only one corner of his mouth up, revealing a dimple in that cheek. I could probably spend hours dissecting his quirks. I doubt I'll have even a minute. He's looking like he wants to find the nearest exit.

Don't leave. I point to his forehead. "Is that a…prop too?"

He touches the wound, then inspects his fingertips. "No. That's from the accident, I guess. We're all a little beat up."

He wipes his fingers on his quilted snow pants. A drop of blood spatters on the black-and-white tile. And I have a flash of déjà vu; it's not the first time I've seen blood on that floor. I swallow my panic, pull a dish towel from the handle of the oven, and toss it to him.

"Thanks," he says, pressing it to his forehead. "Anyway… crazy storm," he says, peering out the window over the sink. I follow his line of vision to the outside. It's probably not even three in the afternoon yet, and already it seems to be getting dark.

He needs to leave, wittle Seda. Stop giving him googly eyes and tell him to get out.

"You should probably get going before it's too late," I tell him, hugging myself.

He grins. "What?"

I stare at him.

"Was that a warning?" he asks, setting his jaw. "What? Do the dead come to life up here after dark?"

"Oh no. I mean, if you want to get somewhere with a phone before it gets dark or the weather gets worse, you'd better go now. We're expecting twenty inches…"

"Honestly, Seda, I think it's already too late," he says conversationally, leaning back against the counter. I am sure I've never looked that comfortable here, even on my very first day. "The Rover's in a ditch. Becca twisted her ankle, and if there's anything worse than a drama queen, it's a drama queen with an actual injury. So we're probably not going anywhere until the storm is over."

He doesn't see how that tears me right down the middle. I

want to help. He's the most life I've seen in forever, beautiful, shining, vibrant *life*. And for that very reason, he doesn't belong here. He only sees the surface right now. But dig a little deeper, and he'll wish he never found us.

Me.

Sawyer.

"I'm sorry. You can't stay here."

He laughs again, like I'm joking. When he realizes I'm serious, a hint of panic taints his pretty voice. "Wait. So what are you saying? You're going to throw us out onto the mountain to die?"

No, I think automatically. *You'll die either way.*

"I know, I know. I'm being overdramatic," he says.

No, that's not what I'm thinking. Actually, the amount of drama was pretty much spot-on.

He continues, "But come on. You're joking, right? Nobody's that heartless."

My stomach is starting to hurt again. I clamp my hands over Sawyer, feeling my blood start to boil as he begins to chant *Don't let the door hit you in the ass, lover boy.* "I'm sorry, but it's really out of the question. It's not…"

Safe. That's the truth. But this boy won't understand that. *Act natural, Seda. Act normal.*

I knew there'd be a time when I'd cross the line and look over my shoulder and not even be able to see where normal once was. Maybe I'm there now. Because every thought swirling in my head feels like it would be strange to him. Finally, I spit out, "Um, you see, we didn't really plan on visitors."

"Well, that's funny, because we really didn't plan on visiting," he says with a smirk. "But if we…"

He trails off when he sees me shaking my head fiercely. "No. You *don't* want to stay here. Believe me. You're better off out there."

"You really think so?" he asks, the bewilderment thick in his voice. "But hear me out. We don't have to stay in the main house. There's a little blue one we passed. Over there? With the weather vane?" He points in the entirely wrong direction, not the first person to succumb to the disorienting effect of Bug House. "That yours too?"

"The carriage house." It's down the drive about half a mile, near Carver Hill Road, and has mostly been consumed by vines and vegetation. I'm surprised the rooster weather vane is still standing because most of the roof has collapsed. Other than having a couple of good walls to brace against the wind, it's not much better than spending the night outside. "Yes."

"With your permission, we'll stay there."

He's fierce, strong, not the type to give in. I, however, collapse like tissue paper under the weight of his pleading brown eyes. "But not for long. Just overnight."

"Thanks," he says, his voice slightly stiff but still pleasant. He's too nice. I might as well have thrown him out on the mountain. Here I am, the girl in a hundred-room mansion, and I can't even offer a few of those rooms to him and his friends during a blizzard?

I am a vile, vile person. But I knew that already.

He doesn't. Not yet. Soon.

I remind myself I'm doing him a favor, keeping him as far away from me—and this house—as possible.

He shoves his hands into his parka and says, "Well. I'd better get back to the others." His eyes travel over to the crystallized package of stew meat thawing on the counter. "Um…"

I'm already shaking my head.

His eyes widen slightly, and he clears his throat. "OK. I'll take that as a no."

"You don't understand," I explain quickly. "It has to last us for I don't know how long. We weren't planning on staying, but my mother decided that she needs to stay here while—"

"Forget it," he says quickly. "I saw a lot of firewood stacked up against the side of the house. Do you have that rationed too?"

I swallow. My mother could look through the trees and see the smoke coming from the chimney. But it'll be dark, and the snow is blowing sideways now in giant smoky waves. I could always say I didn't know they were squatting there. "Take what you need," I find myself saying. "I chopped a lot extra."

He grins, impressed. "*You* did?"

I nod. Well, Sawyer and me, but I'm sure as hell not telling Heath that. I know he thinks I'm mad enough as it is.

7
—

SOME ODDITIES YOU CAN EXPLORE
AT THE HOUSE DURING YOUR STAY:

- The ballroom, where one of the most famous ballerinas in the world is said to have exercised frequently before her untimely "accident." Can you even look at the murals on the wall without getting a distinct case of the willies?
- The nursery and its adjoining schoolroom, where some of our youngest victims spent their nights and days. One has to wonder how anyone slept a wink or learned a single lesson in such creepy quarters!
- The swimming pool, which itself has claimed its share of drowning victims. Don't miss the adjacent exercise room. You may try to exercise your muscles, but we guarantee your nerves will get the better workout!

MY mother is possessed. She hasn't spoken to me since I returned from the freezer, and I can tell she has some amazing idea for her book from the way she's scribbling in her notepad.

She's like this with everything. Once she gets an idea in her head, everything else falls away.

The movie ends, and the screen goes white. Daylight is waning. I turn off the projector and lift the handle for the oil lamp. Out in the hallway, Zoe squeals. A squeal like that means they're all up.

I gather the kids in the room next to the nursery. It looks almost like a real classroom, because somewhere along the line, someone imported four antique classroom desks. They used to have their share of fake cobwebs and blood spatters on them. Adam found a mannequin hand, wrist painted with bright-red "blood," in his desk. There's even a chalkboard on the wall, which used to say GET OUT OR DIE in a frightening scrawl, the final *E* only half formed, suggesting its author had met his untimely demise while trying to write the warning.

Zain sniffles while working on forming the letters of the alphabet. "I want to watch *Nightmare on Elm Street* again."

I put the pencil back in his hand and force him to sit up. "Later."

He sticks out his tongue at me. "I like it when that guy gets sucked into the television and sprayed all over the walls."

I wince. "Yes, that's my favorite part too. Maybe tomorrow."

I sit at the big desk and work on some geometry my mother

had sent over by my new math teacher, Mrs. Paltz, at my high school. Mom wrote to the high school in August to tell them we might be a few weeks late in returning, and could we get a few assignments sent here so I could keep up? Mrs. Paltz sent me a staggering number of assignments, all in a blue binder. I remember thinking I'd never be able to make it through them all. Now, as I page through to the back of the binder, I realize I only have two left.

Looking over the geometry, which might as well be in Chinese, I realize I'm already light-years behind my classmates. I bet kids in the outside world are far better prepared than I am. For what, I don't know. That's how out of it I am. I don't even know what there is to prepare for. College? College seems like traveling to Mars, given how far we are from civilization.

I peer out the window. The snow is still falling; we probably have a good eight inches already. I get up from my seat and peel back the gauzy curtain, searching past the storm and the heavy pine trees separating Bug House from its carriage house.

I wonder what they're doing in there. I wonder if they've taken their SATs yet. I wonder if they know more about geometry than I do. I wonder a million other things about them too.

I imagine their laughter, charged with excitement, in the

whistle of the wind. I imagine them dancing around a fire, immune to the wind's chill. I press my palm flat against the cold, leaded-glass window. It's almost as if I can feel their life force, even from half a mile away.

I wonder if Heath Hunter is thinking about me. I wonder if he knows how odd I am yet.

Of course he does.

At dinner, I slurp my stew as the kids run around the table. I can't help thinking about how I'd turned Heath down when he asked for food. Everything's the same as the dozens of nights that came before this one, except for one thing.

Them. Like so many things in my life, even though they're not here, I can feel them.

They might as well be in the same room as me. Heath Hunter with his easy smile. Those girls with their shining hair. I see them in the brown, watery liquid at the bottom of my bowl.

"What's the problem?" my mother asks suddenly from across the table. "You're not sick, honey, are you?"

"No, nothing's wrong," I lie, slurping more.

I'm not thinking when I tuck the kids into bed. Adam notices—he always notices—because he knocks on my head and asks, "Anyone home?" I pull his blankets up to his chin.

I force myself to laugh as I take off his glasses and put them on the bedside table. "Knock, knock."

"Who's there?" all four kids shriek at once.

"Olive."

"Olive you!" They all giggle.

I need to come up with some new material. But they're an easy audience. They never seem to tire of the same jokes. I kiss their foreheads and slip out the door, then force my feet to climb the stairs to the attic. My feet seem to have more courage than I do. They want to go the other way, to run out into the snow and see our visitors.

But what would I do? Peek through the windows? Spy on them?

I think of Heath Hunter and press back hard on the resulting pain in my stomach. I run my hands through my hair, and it only occurs to me then how greasy it is. I cross my eyes so I can see my nose, which is red and shiny. I probably haven't washed in at least a week. Maybe two. I look like…what had that boy in the store said? Trailer trash.

I scrape at the stain on my Boston College sweatshirt. I'm not from a trailer, but next to them, I feel less…less *everything*.

I need to forget them. I change into my nightgown. I turn off the lights, climb in bed, try to sleep.

It doesn't work. My throat clenches. I stare up at the ceiling and pray I can go to sleep and not dream of drowning for one damn night.

That doesn't work either.

After a while, I get up and look at my snow globes, wondering if I could squeeze myself into those picture-perfect scenes. In the big one, the one of Harvard Square, I see my dark outline, reflected in the glass. I fill in the blanks, and oh yes, that boy is right. Trashy, trashy, trashy.

I get a tissue and wipe my face with it, and run it on my neck and under my armpits. I scrape my hair into a higher ponytail and fluff it.

I practice smiling in a comely way. I still look like something Heath Hunter would find on the bottom of his shoe. I think of that sparkly girl Heath Hunter was with. Becca. She's obviously his girlfriend, because boys like Heath Hunter simply *belong* with girls like that. He said she'd hurt her ankle. He said they couldn't leave until she was better.

But things won't get better here. They need to know that. It'll only get worse.

8

There are no mirrors in our lovely little hotel, and we advise our guests against bringing their own. Doppelgängers have been known to enter the Bismarck-Chisholm House through mirrors, which are portals to another world. These evil beings have been known to imitate guests and create terror and havoc in our hallways. Warning: If you do bring a mirror, even a small one, the doppelgängers will find it! We will not be held responsible if they do.

THERE are no mirrors in Bug House.

No intact ones, at least. My aunt and uncle smashed them and left the frames hanging on the wall, with just a few shards in place.

The brochure says it is because of the doppelgängers. There's an old legend that a mirror is an alternate universe that holds a twin that is, at best, a little naughty, and at worst, downright evil. Sometimes a twin will come in through the mirror at night and make mischief, like rearranging your shoes or moving your car keys. But evil ones have been known to murder their twins, hide the bodies, and take their place in this world. The legend says that if a person is a doppelgänger, like a vampire, he will have no reflection in a mirror.

In the upstairs bathroom though, there are a few remnants of a mirror, a triangle-shaped piece of glass still attached to the medicine cabinet.

I make my trips there as quick as possible. I only go in to do my business and get out. And I never look into that mirror. Never.

But this time, I stand in the doorway, listening to the maddening *drip, drip, drip* of the water into the claw-foot bathtub. Three steps in. Three steps out. That's all.

I can do it.

I run in, focused only on that little, white handle above the pedestal sink. My fingers close around it. Yanking the cabinet open, I grab a roll of gauze, some tape, and some antibiotic. I slam the door shut in one swift movement, about to make this the quickest bathroom trip in the history of bathroom trips.

But then my eyes catch on that triangle of glass.

My reflection. My real one this time, not just a distorted shadow in glass.

It is so stark, so shocking. I cringe in horror. Maybe it'd

be better if I were a doppelgänger. Then I wouldn't have to see myself. I've lost more weight, so my cheeks look like I'm consciously sucking in air. My hair used to be blondish, but now it's nearly black, with an oily sheen over it.

People used to say I looked more and more like my mother every day. I'm her mini-me, after all.

My lips move without me intending it. *You're nothing like her anymore. You're a monster.*

I pile the medical supplies against my chest and steal out of the room. I don't know what time it is. Later than bedtime, which is eight o'clock. That's not very late, I guess, but it's always been that way here. Since it gets dark early, it's better to be asleep.

That's why I feel strange as I walk down the darkened staircase, almost as if I'm somewhere foreign. The hulking grandfather clock looks like a hunched old man, watching me as I grab my cape off the coatrack and steal across the foyer. The clock's ticking sounds like, *Go back, go back, go back.* Every noise feels like a warning.

But I need this. Like my mother constantly says, sometimes we need to shake up our routine so we don't go stir-crazy. And it would be nice to prove I'm still a real teen, a real part of this world.

Go ahead, Sawyer taunts. *It might be the last chance you get.*

My footsteps echo as I push open the swinging door to the kitchen. I turn on the light. It is shockingly bright.

I find the key to the freezer in the tea canister. I know what I am looking for. Otherwise I'm sure I would chicken out. I tell myself that what I have to do will take only one breath's time, and it does, because I hold my breath the entire time. I turn the key, twist the latch, and pull it open—*Pop!* Then I reach inside and yank the hot dogs from the shelf.

The cartoon hot dog on the package smiles toothily, promising goodness within. All lies, according to my mother. The dogs are organic and uncured and have all the stuff that's supposed to make them taste good. But my mom read an article that said the labels aren't truthful, and even so-called organic hot dogs are full of nitrites. We only have them because Zoe begged for them—throwing herself on the floor when Mom wouldn't buy them—then promptly, after half a nibble, declared them *gross*.

I stuff everything into a canvas shopping bag. Throwing my cape over my back, I scuff my feet into the heavy duck boots I'd left on the mat, then look down at myself. My checkered flannel nightgown stretches from neck to toe, and it's as red as my cape and my flushed cheeks. I'll probably look like the Red Death, coming after them at the masquerade party.

But if they pry off my mask, what they see will be even worse than a plague. I stifle a maniacal laugh as I quietly shove open the door and am hit by a wall of icy wind. This *is* crazy.

But they need me, I tell myself, clutching the bag against my chest. I bring them sustenance and valuable supplies.

The wind is not as bad on the side of the house, where the building blocks the chill blasting over the lake behind the house. The snow has almost stopped. It's just an odd flake here or there, and the surface of the snow glints like silver. The bony tree limbs scrape at the full moon now poking out from the cloud canopy. I plod along through the snow, which is up to my calves, hoping my mother doesn't pick tonight to come to check on me in my room.

The whistle of the wind through the trees is the only sound I hear as I approach the carriage house. When it comes into view, I see the warm orange glow of fire.

A girl laughs, high-pitched and vibrant.

I stop in my tracks, contemplating whether I should invade. No, probably not. Sounds like they're making do just fine on their own.

Something makes me inch closer anyway. Their life force is a magnet I'm inexplicably drawn to. There are three remaining walls, and while almost all the windows have been boarded up, there's a large space between the wooden slats. I climb over the snowdrifts and holly brambles and peek inside.

Four of them are sitting around a fire they've built in the center of the room. Heath Hunter's face is shining bright and vibrant in the dim light. He looks so confident, so strong, a small smile of amusement on his face. He has his arm around the blond-haired girl, who is curled up to him with her head under his chin. Even though she's covered in a blanket, she's visibly shivering.

They're all watching one of the boys—the Mountain Dew guy from Art's—standing over them. He holds up his hand as if delivering a toast.

All at once, the room erupts into laughter. What an odd sound. The other girl whistles and says something that sounds like, *Shut up, dumbass.* The other one—he's facing away from me—balls something up in his hands and throws it at Mountain Dew guy. He puts up his hands in surrender and saunters back to the fire. "What can I say? I like them hot," he says, sitting himself down.

Who are these people? How can they be so sure of themselves? How can they not sense the danger? How can they not feel the weight of the moments ticking by? The longer they stay here, the more the dark energy of this mountain will make itself known. The more impossible it will be to leave.

The only one who *maybe* gets it is the girl curled around Heath. She's staring at the fire, oblivious to all of them, her face rigid.

My hand curls around the canvas bag. I look down at its meager contents. What good will hot dogs and bandages do now? None.

They need to leave. I need to get them to leave.

Suddenly, the blond girl starts to shriek. She sits up, pin straight, staring through the slats, right at me. She points. "There's someone out there! Oh my God! There's a face! A ghost!"

She starts to scoot backward on the floor, throwing off her blanket. It's not a blanket; it's Heath's coat, I realize as I back away from the window. Tripping over the brambles, I fall butt first into the snow. By the time I stand up and start to break into a run, someone comes around the side of the house. "Hey!"

I stop. I turn.

Heath Hunter.

"Well, hello, Seda Helm," he says with that easy smile of his. His hands are stuffed in the pockets of his snow pants, and he's wearing a thermal shirt that defines his chest. His sleeves are rolled up to the elbows, despite the cold, and his exposed skin is a pleasant shade of tan. "You go peeking in windows like that, and people are bound to think you're a ghost. You're as pale as one anyway."

My face heats. "I'm sorry." I hold out the canvas bag and then toss it to him. It lands by his feet. "I brought you some things."

He swipes it off the snowy ground, but his eyes never leave mine. "That's all well and good, Seda Helm, but what about you?"

The way he says my name makes it feel musical and almost as special as his. His gaze sends a chill down my body. Has anyone ever looked at me like that before? "Me?"

He nods. "You're going to go back to that big house of yours without allowing us the pleasure of your company?"

I stand there, shivering in my cape and flannel nightgown.

He motions me to follow. "Come on. It's the least you can do after scaring poor Becca to death."

Now that's something I'm probably good at. Filling my lungs with icy air, I tramp along the edge of the house, steadying myself against the cold stone wall until I'm close to him.

He grins down at me. "I feel like the Big Bad Wolf."

"Huh?"

He touches the sleeve of my felt cape. "Little Red Riding Hood? 'All the better to eat you with, my dear?'"

I shudder.

"I'm kidding," he says. "Do they not joke around here?"

My heart is beating a million miles an hour. "Oh, they do," I say lightly, trying to preserve my dignity. I try to think of some witty joke or retort to show him what kidders we are, but the only thing that sticks in my mind is the "Olive you" knock-knock joke I use on the kids, and that's definitely not right. I really do need new material.

He leads me back into the carriage house, through the crumbling front wall. The place smells like pine and musty earth and burning wood. Four faces watch me as I step over a fallen ceiling beam onto a floor that is more pine needles and dirt than stone. Heath Hunter presents me to the group, which is huddled around a makeshift fire pit. "This is Seda Helm," he says. "She lives on this property."

I fight back the nausea bubbling in my throat as they inspect me.

"Seda Helm, this is Mike Whitman, whom we call Wit. Captain of Shady View swim and the fastest freestyler in the state." Mountain Dew guy narrows his eyes at me.

Heath continues the introductions. "That's Liam over there." I sweep my eyes toward the fire as I remember what he'd said at Art's. *Yes, here I am, inbred trash girl, in all my glory.* "He… What is it you do again, Li?"

"Screw off," Liam grunts, picking up his GoPro and pointing

it at me. "Here we have the girl who lives on this haunted property, and over there"—he points the camera at Heath—"is a massive jerkwad."

"I love you too." Heath juts a chin toward the dark-haired girl with the devil horns. "That's Liam's baby sister, Astrid, and—"

"Watch who you're calling *baby*," she snarls at him. Truthfully, the girl is broad-faced, broad-bodied, and obviously pretty solid, even without the white puffer coat she's wearing. She looks like she can take care of herself. "I'm only four months younger than him, and four days older than *you*."

Heath gives her a playful smirk. "Whatever."

She mutters to me, "You don't have to be Sherlock to see we're not related by blood. Our parents adopted me from China when I was a baby." It's clear from how annoyed she sounds that she's been explaining that all her life.

Heath finishes, "And over there is Becca."

Becca is the girl with the pink and blue pigtails. She leans in toward the fire, and the black heart on her cheek crinkles upward. "Thanks, girl," she mutters, nursing her injured ankle. "I needed the heart attack. Really."

Astrid snorts. "So, you're the one who lives in that big house? And you couldn't even let us in to use the bathroom?

Nice. I had to squat in the woods. Nearly got a pinecone up my ass."

It's as if their eyes are knives, cutting into me the way Sawyer is always cutting into me from the inside. I fidget from foot to foot. "Oh. Well, I'd better go."

Heath Hunter nearly lunges to stop me. "Hey, guys. Lighten up." He opens the canvas supply bag, pulls out the ACE bandage, and tosses it to Becca. "She brought rations."

Becca snorts, less than appreciative. "Great, rations. What is this for?" she snaps.

I look at her, surprised. Heath quickly interjects. "Your ankle. Remember?" He shakes his head. "What, has the cold frozen your brain?"

She glares at him, then at me. "Oh right."

Wit is the first one to come to my defense. I guess he's feeling guilty for Liam having called me trailer trash. "Yeah, come on, dudes." He looks at me and smiles. "So your parents have a short leash on you? Hunter told us all about it."

"Um, just my mom," I push out, my teeth suddenly chattering from the cold. "My dad…"

I trail off like I usually do whenever he comes up.

"Come on," Heath Hunter says, nudging me toward the fire. "Take a load off. Get warm."

This is a bad idea. But there's something in the way he looks at me that makes me agree. He sits down on a collapsed ceiling rafter and pats the spot next to him. I sit there, close but not quite touching him. When I look up, Becca is staring at me.

"Heath," she says, holding out the bandage. "Are you going to help me with this or what?"

He stands and makes his way over to her. She holds out a dainty, fishnet-stocking-covered foot, and he starts to wrap it. "Just call me Florence Nightingale," he says, winking at me. I watch them, rapt. She is so cool and collected as he touches her skin. Evan never had a chance to touch me before I left. I'm sure I'd jump a thousand miles into the air if anyone touched me like that.

When he finishes, Heath gently pulls her snow-pant leg down and fixes her bulky sock over the injured ankle. I think the last time I saw such chivalry, we were in Boston, when my father would pull my mother's feet in his lap and rub them after a long day at the college. Somehow, the thought brings a tear to my eye as I watch Becca rest her head on Heath's shoulder and pull his coat up to her chin. She shudders as another gust of wind hits the house, rattling the remaining glass in the windowpanes. "This wind is ridiculous," she mutters.

It's actually not that cold right in front of the fire. It's cozy.

Strange that this crumbling wreck of a building feels cozier than Bug House ever has. I pull the hood off my head and lean into the warmth.

"So, little Red," Heath Hunter says, leaning over and tapping me on my foot. "Tell us all about yourself."

Now I know why this is a bad idea. Liam and Wit are intermittently pelting each other with pinecones. Astrid plucks imaginary lint from her fuzzy scarf, and Becca is scooting so close to Heath that she's nearly on his lap, miserably seeking out more warmth. The only one staring at me, the only one who wants to hear my life story, is Heath Hunter.

"There's not much to tell," I mumble.

He scratches the side of his jaw. "OK, Silent One. But this place…this place speaks volumes. How long have you lived here?"

"Since June."

Liam stops, picks up his GoPro, and points it at me. "And you've survived that long?"

I bristle. "What do you mean?"

Astrid scoffs and runs her fingers through her black hair. "Duh. He means that this place is totally creepy. I heard stories about it when I was at camp. It's haunted, right?"

I shake my head. "It's not. It was a murder house. You know, murder mystery dinners and weekends and stuff? But we're going to sell it and move back to Boston." I swallow. "Eventually."

"Really?" Wit pipes up, stretching out his long, scarecrow legs. "What are you waiting for?"

"We're still looking for a buyer."

Becca lets out a short laugh. "You really think anybody would buy that place?"

Suddenly I feel cold. "Well, my mother is particular about who buys it. We had an offer, but they were going to tear it down to build a ski resort. My mother thinks it should be preserved. But my…" I stop. Back to my dad again. Funny how all roads lead back to him. I remember what he'd told my mother: *You had an offer, and you let it go? Maya, they could turn this place into a junkyard for all I care.* He'd been so angry at her. God, I'd never seen my dad so angry.

Heath Hunter's eyes haven't left my face, and it's borderline creepy and humiliating having someone staring at me like that. I'm glad the fire is so warm because I can blame the heat in my cheeks on that. "Did you inherit it from a crazy old uncle or something?"

Becca nudges him as if he's said something inappropriate and offensive, but I'm not sure why, since she doesn't strike me as a person who would care. I nod, surprised at how perceptive he is. "We're from Boston," I say again, a hint of pride in my voice. I'm not the backwoods girl they thought. I had quite the metropolitan upbringing. Not that they look very impressed. "My mom's a writer. Well, she's also a professor at Boston College. But she took a sabbatical after last term and now she's working from here, writing, while we wait for the place to sell. She says it's good inspiration for the book she's writing."

That gets their attention. Even Astrid, who I can tell is easily bored, raises an eyebrow. Wit pushes his glasses up on his nose and says, "Really? Cool. Is she writing a horror novel?"

"No. It's nonfiction. She specializes in horror movies though."

"Has she been published?"

I nod. "Well, for now, she's only published articles and stuff. She had one piece published in the *Boston Globe*. About—"

"How much she wanted to live in a shithole?" Liam interjects.

I shake my head, thinking of the piece. It was a short history and guide to the horror movie genre, which might sound exciting at first, but I've read the first few pages, and it reads like a school textbook. If anyone can make slasher films sound like high art, it's my mom.

Becca suddenly clutches at her stomach. "Ugh. Listen to that, will you? It sounds like a wild animal is digging its way out!" She moans in agony.

I think of Sawyer. He has been so silent all this time, as if he's been waiting, sizing them up.

"I brought hot dogs," I offer, lifting the canvas bag. I dig around in it and pull out the plastic-wrapped package.

One by one, they all catch sight of the hot dogs and break out in hysterics. I feel like I am missing out on the punch line of a great joke, and the more they laugh, the more I'm reminded that I am and always will be the outsider.

Heath Hunter recovers from his laughter and says, "Now I know I'm in hell."

I stare. This place *does* look like hell, but why is he laughing about it?

Wit points to the package, where it says HUNTER HOT DOGS. Then he points to Heath Hunter. He says, "So this man forgot to tell you that he is the Wiener Prince of Pennsylvania?"

Heath picks a stick off the ground and chucks it at him, a close-lipped smile on his face. "Shut it, Stretch." He reaches over and takes the package from me. His voice is soft. "My father owns this factory. And these assholes will never let me live it down." He fake-scowls at each of them in turn.

"I'm sorry," I say, reaching for the hot dogs.

"No, hell no." Becca grabs the package and starts to tear it open with her teeth. "I am eating *all of these*."

"I think there's a joke in there somewhere, but I'm too hungry to think of it," Wit mutters. Then he pretends to lunge for her. "Give me those dogs or die!"

She pulls them away and squeals. "Get away from me, creep."

But they're all laughing. He tumbles on top of her, making her squeal even louder. Astrid grabs the package and yanks it away, and Wit bear-hugs her. She manages to toss the hot dogs back to Becca before he can put his hands on them. Liam reaches for them but does a completely ungraceful swan dive over a fallen rafter and lands with a thud and a *dammit!*

Everyone's smiling, but that's not the weirdest thing that's ever happened on this mountain. The strangest part is that I find myself smiling too.

Heath leans over Becca with his big arms and easily yanks the hot dogs out of her grasp. "I guess I'll have to dole them out. One per customer." Then he winks at me again and leans in close, so close that I can feel his breath on my cheek.

"If you won't let us stay with you, at least stay with us," he whispers in my ear.

9

Being scared to death is only half the fun. Every stay at the Bismarck-Chisholm House includes a one-of-a-kind mystery that guests must solve in order to "survive" their stay. Work together with or compete against other guests—it's up to you. All survivors leave with a special commemorative pin and a certificate, as well as bragging rights. Not many people can say, "I survived Bismarck-Chisholm!" Will you be one of them?

IT'S like I'm having an out-of-body experience. I see myself sitting next to the fire and watching these people my age talking and laughing, and I almost feel like I'm the girl who used to hang out in Rachel's brownstone, talking about normal teen things. It's like these past couple of months of isolation are being erased before my very eyes.

Heath Hunter hands me a stick with a charred hot dog on it. I pry it off and take a bite, and then another, like I haven't eaten in days. I don't care if nitrites are going to kill me; it's delicious.

"Easy, Red," he says to me, making me blush.

There is a nervous feeling in the group though, because while they're laughing and joking, they keep glancing out the broken windows. It isn't any more unease than I'm used to feeling, that's for certain, which is why I'm almost comfortable here, despite the icy glances the girls keep giving me.

Becca seems less miserable with a full belly. She gives me a smile and says, "Thanks for the dogs." Then she rubs her mittened hands together. "So do you think we'll be able to get out of here tomorrow?"

Heath Hunter shrugs. "Snow's stopped. We should be able to get down the mountain, and then maybe we can flag a passing car."

He looks at me to give a thumbs-up to his plan, but I can't. Carver Hill Road doesn't see any traffic but us. The more major road they're talking about, Rural Route 9, is probably the one they slid off. It's a mile downhill and so treacherous that it closes for the season, or so I heard Elmer say once. Most people take the freeway if they're going to the ski resorts.

"I don't think there will be anyone on that road," I say. "Honestly, we don't get anyone coming out this way. You guys are the first."

Now Becca is back to looking like she wants to kill me. Maybe I should've lied?

Liam groans and starts to film his crumbling surroundings.

"'Let's take the scenic road,' they said. 'It'll be fun,' they said,"
he mimics. "Just remember, I was the one who told you to take
the freeway. If it weren't for you guys wanting to Robert Frost
it with your stupid *road less traveled* idea, we'd be sipping hot
cocoa in the lodge."

"Yeah, you're brilliant, bro," Astrid mutters. "Shut up."

"Well, it *has* made all the difference," Wit quips, and I can
tell from the resulting groans that everyone wants to throw
something at him. Only Heath Hunter does: someone's glove.
He pelts him in the chin.

"What kind of house doesn't even have a phone?" Becca
grouses, giving me an accusing glare. As if I'm the one who
decided that Bug House wouldn't have any connection to the
outside world. "This is insane. I mean, what are we going to
do…stay stuck here for the rest of the winter?"

Her voice is rising steadily, getting more and more frantic.
Heath Hunter holds up his palms. "Hey, hey, hey. Just wait.
We're not going to be stuck here forever. It's only October 31.
The snow will melt. If worse comes to worst, I'll hike out to the
nearest business, which is…" He looks at me.

"Art's," I fill in.

He raises an eyebrow. "That place we got rations? Seriously?
That's like…ten miles away?"

"Twenty."

He looks down at his feet. "Shit." Then he starts rubbing his hands together. "That's OK. Hell, I ran a marathon last year. Twenty miles is nothing. Even with snow. It's fine."

"Our parents will be worrying about us," Astrid puts in.

The rest of them look at her doubtfully.

She looks at Liam for confirmation. "Well, we told ours we'd call the second we got up there. When we don't, they'll call the police. And they'll find the Land Rover. Maybe we should've stayed with it."

Liam shakes his head. "We'd freeze there overnight. The temps are below freezing. And the police won't find the Land Rover because they'll think we went on the interstate. They'll think we had better sense than to go the bass-ackward way we went. I mean, you two dean's list jerks are too smart for that."

Becca scowls at him. "What are you talking about? We didn't even apply to colleges yet."

"Yeah, man," Heath Hunter mutters. "You trying to jinx us?"

Wit starts to dig at the fire with a stick, and Becca sighs, her face sick. "I think we're jinxed enough as it is. We'll probably never get out of here. Come spring, they'll find nothing but our bones."

Astrid punches her shoulder. "Get. A. Grip."

Liam exhales. "Maybe it's better that way." He looks at Astrid. "Dad's going to have my head when he sees what I did to the Rover."

She nods sullenly in agreement. "Right. Right. The Rover was trashed. Forget letting us go to Florida for spring break."

"Guys! We're fine. But we can't do anything about the Land Rover right now, so there's no use thinking about it," Heath Hunter says, leaning back on his elbows. "So let's take it easy and stop playing the what-if game, projecting grim outcomes that aren't going to happen."

Wit snorts. "Sure, let's sing songs. Anyone got a harmonica? We can have a party. A Donner party."

They all start to laugh, even Becca. I smile along, feeling that same nervous excitement I used to whenever I'd hang with my friends in Boston. Becca shakes her pigtails and twirls one of them between her fingers. She licks her lips and inspects her pink fingernails. I study her, registering her every move so that I can imitate them later. So that I can be a Typical Girl My Age. I know I'm borderline gawking, which probably isn't polite, but I can't help it. Eventually she looks over at me and scowls. Then she leans in and whispers, "Take a picture. It'll last longer."

Just then, the wind hits the side of the house, releasing a

low, subhuman moaning. Becca shudders. Astrid says, "That's the dead girl."

Everyone looks at her.

"Oh my God, you guys never heard the stories? We used to tell them all the time when I went to camp." She grins at me. "The people who owned this house before you. A couple and their daughter. One night the man went berserk and chopped them all to pieces with an ax."

I cringe.

Liam says, "This place does have a *The Shining* vibe to it." He looks at me. "Hey, you said your mom was a writer. Is she eccentric? Does she ever stare at her computer screen obsessively?"

I swallow. Yes, and all the time. I've read the brochure about the house. When we moved in, there were dozens of them scattered all over the foyer, under an inch-thick layer of dust. They said, *Welcome to the most haunted mansion in Allegheny County. The legend of this home says that no one has ever been able to live here through the winter without succumbing to the disorienting effect of Solitude Mountain...*

But those are simply stories, like all those plaques in the hallways. The lore was all made up to go with the murder house theme.

"That's one of the story lines they used in the games they

ran," I explain. "My aunt and uncle lived here before. They never had any kids."

Astrid gives me a mischievous smile. "That's a boring campfire story. I like mine better. Who did *they* buy it from?"

I shrug. Wit scratches his jaw and studies me so closely that I feel my cheeks blaze. "I like Astrid's story better too. Maybe *you're* the daughter, come back to haunt us." He leans over and touches the sleeve of my nightgown with his index finger. "Nope. Solid as a rock."

Heath snorts. "Yeah. I've heard of that. Ghosts like to make their presence known by either rattling chains or bringing hot dogs."

The rest of them laugh, but Liam says, glaring into the fire, "Screw the ghosts. I don't doubt that it happened. The fact is, a place like this, like the Overlook Hotel in *The Shining*, has a way of making people who are only borderline crazy full-on psychotic. Places like this bring out the demons in all of us."

His voice is so low and ominous that I shudder. *Borderline crazy.*

Like me.

Becca lets out a squeal. "Can you shut up? Stop trying to creep me out. I'm already creeped out enough as it is."

"You don't have to be." The lie bursts out of me so quickly

that I can't reel it back in. Every head in the room turns to look at me.

"So you've never seen anything creepy here?" Becca asks, studying the eaves of the house where the roof hasn't caved in. Little flakes of snow have begun to fall from the sky again, drifting into our warm nook and landing delicately on her shoulders.

"No. Nothing. It's only a house—four walls and a roof. We're…" I swallow. "We're all very happy here."

I study each of their faces in the firelight's warm glow. They're so silly. They seem disappointed that Bug House is not infested with ghosts.

But there *is* strange energy here, and it'll rip through them, one by one. I can feel it, and I'm afraid. The truth is, there are worse things that can happen to a home than a haunting.

10

Ghost stories involving the Bismarck-Chisholm House are the stuff of local legends. But some of those legends are true. Perhaps you heard of the previous owner who went insane and murdered his entire family? Edwin Smith hacked his daughter and wife to death with an ax one lonely winter in 1973, before hanging himself in an upstairs bedroom. The grisly murders were only discovered the following spring. The only surviving member of their immediate family? One of the family dogs who made it through the winter by eating the corpses of its dead family.

ONE by one, they all begin to yawn and fall back on their duffel bags, settling in for the night. The firelight dims, and the wind dies down. An ache, dull at first, blooms in my stomach, growing thick tendrils that wind their way up to my chest, squeezing at my heart.

He's coming on stronger now.

I have to go. I've been here too long.

I stand up and wipe the pine needles from my backside. Heath raises an eyebrow, then gets up to meet me. Becca opens an eye and stares at me blankly. "I need to go," I whisper.

Heath Hunter says, "OK. I'll walk you back."

I don't know why that makes my spirits lift. It's not wise for him to come too close to the house, because my mother might see him and invite them in, and then I'll be under the same roof with them. No matter how much I enjoy Heath's company, I need distance.

It's snowing again. Not lightly either. The flakes are blowing sideways and pelting our faces. I bury my face in my cape so I can't see his, but I'm sure it doesn't register worry. He isn't even wearing a coat. He keeps moving against the weather, whistling a cheery rendition of "Ride of the Valkyries," which I only recognize because my mom can never write to anything but classical music. I can already tell Heath Hunter doesn't get worried by much.

As we walk, he scrapes up some snow with his bare hands and makes a snowball. "Anyway, thanks for the dogs," he says. "Sorry about those guys."

I cock my head at him. "Why are you sorry?"

"Well, they weren't very appreciative of what you did. But for the record, I am."

I shake my head. "I wish I could do more. I should. I mean…it's hard, but I can't explain."

He nods as if he understands, but how could he possibly understand? "I got it, I got it. Your mom is a little controlling, huh? My parents are too. They send me off to boarding school, so I have the illusion of freedom. But I'm not free, really. You see, I have to go to Stanford for business so I can inherit my destiny as the Wiener King. There can be no deviation from that plan."

"They want the best for you," I say softly. "My mom too."

"Yeah. Sure. That's why you won't catch me complaining."

Oh. I didn't mean to imply that he was. "My mom is big on protecting us. Me. She's also a little…out there. Typical writer type. And I guess she feels guilty about my father—"

I freeze and shudder as my mind lurches to the last time I saw my dad. My parents had a lot of screaming matches, but none fiercer than those during Dad's last few days here. They were always putting me in the middle of their arguments, as if I were their marriage counselor, the wise person who could smooth all their conflicts, and not a kid who'd never even had a date with the opposite sex. The last thing my dad ever said to me echoes in my head: *Tell her to call me if you can talk some sense into her.*

My stomach roils, which has nothing to do with Sawyer. I look at Heath. He has a kind face, like my dad's. Snow is crusting over his hair and eyebrows, and my goodness, he must be cold. But he's not complaining. He's studying me like he's really interested in what I have to say next. It's a new experience for me, so I blush and forget whatever I was going to say.

"Is he gone now?"

I swallow. I don't want to talk about my dad. Don't want to talk about them. "He met us up here for our last week of summer vacation. But he hated this place from the start. When my mother admitted she'd been stalling about selling this place, he was furious. He left. One morning I woke up, and he was gone. I haven't talked to him since. I mean, we can't. There's no phone service. So…" I trail off. There's really nothing else to say.

"Seriously?" Heath shakes his head. I pray he won't ask me more, and he doesn't. He simply mumbles, "That's messed up."

He changes the subject by pointing through a break in the stone wall and down a snow-covered path that cuts through the woods. "Hey, is that a graveyard over there?"

I don't even look. Don't want to.

"Um. No. Cemetery, actually."

He grins. "Same difference, right?"

I shake my head. "Graveyards usually belong to a church."

My stomach twists as the words leave my mouth. I mean, these people already think I'm weird. Now that he knows I'm an expert on where people bury their dead, he must think I'm completely psycho.

"Really?" He starts to backtrack that way, but I tuck my head down and pick up the pace to the house. "Hey. What's wrong?"

"I don't go there. Cemeteries creep me out."

"Who's buried there? People who once lived at the house?"

"Maybe. I don't know. The headstones might not even be real. That's the thing about this place. There's a lot that isn't what it seems. You never know what is real and what's not. It all *looks* real, at least."

"Cool." That's what my mother says, and the reason she doesn't want this place going to any old buyer. He catches my dubious expression and says, "I know it's morbid. But even if it isn't real, I like old burial places. I like walking through them."

"You like walking over dead people?"

He laughs. "I like the quiet. But when you put it that way... actually, they suck. What was I thinking?"

I can't help it. I smile.

"Why do you do that?" he asks.

"What?"

"Cover your mouth with your hand when you smile. Don't you like it?"

My face falls. I press my lips together and force my hand to my side. I hadn't noticed I do that. It just happens naturally. But obviously he noticed. Something tells me not much escapes Heath Hunter. "What, smiling?"

"No. Your mouth."

"It's not that. It's—" *It's just that it's so unfamiliar to have my mouth twist that way that I'm self-conscious.* "I don't know."

"Is it because you have braces?" He grins. "I like braces. I think they're cute. Let me see."

I swallow the lump in my throat. "What do you mean?"

"Open up."

My lips spread apart, despite my better judgment. It's like every part of my body is eager to do what he asks. He studies my mouth like a dentist. "Cute."

Not really. I'd gotten my braces late enough as it was, when I was thirteen. I was supposed to get them off in August. Now I'll probably have the straightest teeth in the world, since who knows when I'll get back to my orthodontist in Boston. I don't want to talk about my weirdness anymore. "I think the snow-storm might be over."

He laughs again. "Yeah. We keep saying that. I think Becca will go a little batty if we don't get off this mountain soon. Sorry if she was mean to you."

"It's OK. I understand."

"Do you? Because I really don't. I mean, we broke up two years ago. But she's a drama queen, literally. I mean, she's had a starring role in every Shady View school play since she got to high school, so even she'd tell you she isn't entirely comfortable unless the spotlight is on her. So every time I talk to a pretty girl, she puts up the bitch defense."

Pretty girl. Is he referring to me? Dirty hair, ratty nightgown, braces, and all? My heart skips at least a dozen beats. Nobody has ever called me pretty. But before I can think of a way to respond, he's already moved on.

"So, what's this big old house out here in the middle of nowhere for, do you think?"

Teeth chattering, part from the cold and part in response to the pretty-girl comment, I tell him what I've learned—from what I've heard and read, and from my googling before we lost our internet connection. "It used to be an inn for travelers on their way to Lake Erie," I tell him. "But it got cut off by the railroad. And then nobody came. A long time ago, the owners started adding on different wings and secret passages and stuff like that. My brothers and sisters love it. I think I would too if I were younger."

"Right, you said you have brothers and sisters?"

I nod. "All younger than me. Two sets of twins, four and six years old."

"Wow. Two sets? That's nuts. They must be good kids. I didn't hear anyone making noise when I was in the house. That's why I thought it was deserted."

"It was their nap time," I explain.

"Ah."

We get to the back door to the kitchen. Something is happening to my body, making me feel dizzy and warm despite the cold. I know I've never felt this before, but I'm certain my heart will miss him the second he's gone. I feel bad, leaving him and his friends to that crumbling old shack with nothing more than a few hot dogs and some gauze.

I glance back at the door and then lean in and whisper, "Noises don't carry in the house. It's too big. Someone could scream at the top of their lungs from the kitchen, and you wouldn't be able to hear it from my bedroom."

He studies me, his eyes narrowing like I'm the most bewitching creature he's ever seen. I can't stop myself. The words keep coming out, even though I know this is a mistake. Them, inside? Sneaking around, so close to… *Forget it, Seda. It doesn't matter. Everything will be fine.* Besides, I can no more stop my mouth from running around him than I can help the blush on my cheeks. "And sometimes we forget to lock the house, since we're up here on the mountain, all alone," I finish.

A small smile spreads on his face. He gets my not-so-subtle hint.

He reaches out and takes my hand under the cape. Amazingly, though he has no coat to bury them in, his hands are still warmer than mine. His fingers entwine with mine. "Thanks, Seda. Good night."

11

Fancy a stroll around our grounds? Misty Lake, mere steps away, is peaceful to look at, but don't bother casting your lines. No fish have ever been caught there. The carriage house is where famous murderer Rusty Joe lived. The pitchfork-welding groundskeeper killed several guests in the summer of 1958. Briar Cemetery, hidden among the woods on the east end of the property, is where many of the guests who died here have been buried. It's quite crowded now, but don't worry —we always have room for one more!

ANOTHER day dawns gray and murky, the same as so many others that have come before it. When I lift myself out of bed, I look around the room and rub a knot in my neck.

I'd say I slept badly, but the truth is, I didn't sleep at all. All night long, I'd listened to that unearthly moaning, thinking of the stories of the dead girl. I imagined a girl screaming as her father chased her and her mother through the dark hallways and secret passages. I watched the shadows of the mannequin pieces swaying in the draft, illuminated by the dullest shaft of moonlight. Their stiff toes and spindly fingers cast shadows from their bizarre canopy in the rafters. I thought about Heath Hunter.

Too much.

And it's so silly, because now that it's morning he'll be gone, taking advantage of the break in the weather to hike back down the mountain with his friends. Gone, leaving the dismal solitude behind. The winter ice will probably be thawing again before I see another human being outside of our family.

I sigh, pull off my flannel nightgown, and slip into a fresh sweatshirt, then catch a look at my snow globes. They're shining brighter than ever. I realize it's because they're reflecting light from outside. Scuttling toward the window, I push aside a shutter and peer at a drift that seems to bury a skeletal tree in the backyard. The snow is still driving down, whiting out most of the scenery beyond the lake.

I only realize I'm pressing my nose against the window when my breath fogs it up. I close the shutter, strip off my sweatshirt, and find my blue bathrobe. Then I clomp noisily down the shaky spiral staircase, take a few deep breaths, and step into the bathroom.

I pull back the black shower curtain around the enormous

claw-foot tub like I'm ripping off a Band-Aid, half expecting something terrible to happen. It doesn't. It's only a tub, after all, the bottom red with rust. I flip the hot and cold handles, waiting for water.

All I get is moaning.

I groan. I need to take a shower. Suddenly, it's a mad desire. I need to strip off layers of this place, to feel human again.

But Bug House obviously has other ideas.

Sighing, I knot my greasy hair on top of my head. I rush down the stairs, peeking from the staircase landing through the windows to the snow-swept forest that lies beyond.

"Can you believe it's still snowing?"

Mom's cheery voice is nothing like the eerie, ghostly whispers that I'm sure my aunt and uncle filled this place with years ago. Even so, I jump clear to the ceiling. I lose my balance for a moment, and my feet slip to the next step before I steady myself against the railing.

"Oh. No," I say, my smile dissolving.

"See, honey?" she says as I reach the first floor, hip checking me as she dances toward the kitchen. I can smell the pancakes cooking, so I know she's made a big, hearty breakfast to go with the weather. "Told you you'd love the winter up here."

"The pipes are frozen, I think," I say.

She tilts her head. "That's nothing a strong hair dryer can't put right."

"I feel all greasy. I need to take a shower."

She seems surprised. It's the first time I've sounded like my Boston self in a long time. Her smile broadens, and she rubs my shoulder. "OK, hon. I'll be up after breakfast."

I'm not listening. I'm looking out the front window toward the carriage house. There might be more than twenty inches out there, given how the snow has buried all the stout holly trees in front of the house.

"Do you think Route 9 is closed?"

Mom raises her eyebrow. I think maybe I've said too much, given away my secret, so I add, "It's just freaky, thinking we've been cut off from everything and everyone."

"Oh. Well, don't worry about that," she says, coming up close to me and kissing my forehead. "We have everything we need. And more, right? We have more love than we know what to do with. It's bursting from the walls."

She grins broadly. There was a time when my dad used to be the one with the stupid jokes, always the one to lighten a room. But he must have left all the levity in the family with my mom. The last few times I talked to my dad, he didn't sound like he was in a joking mood, almost like this place had drained the good humor out of him. "But they close that road, right? When the weather is really bad?"

She nods. "Come on, honey. Have breakfast. I've been thinking more about the *H-U-N-T*." She always spells things like it's a code only the two of us can understand, even though Adam knows full well what she's talking about. "I've been thinking up clues all night!"

Slowly I remember our talk yesterday. "Oh yeah. Sounds fun," I say, my voice dull. Like I said, it will be fun for the young ones. Not for me.

"Are you all right, dear?"

"Oh, fine." I rub my hands together, though I know my cheeks are warm and red and probably giving away my lie. I grab my cape off the coatrack. "It's cold. I should go get more firewood before the snow gets too deep."

"Of course. I'll put on your pancakes for you."

I step into my duck boots, throw my cape over my head, and rush across the dining room, where all four of my siblings scream my name in unison before continuing with their regular mealtime havoc. I give them a half wave and push open the swinging door to the kitchen, then take a deep breath and pull open the door to the outside.

The biting wind hits me before I'm outside, stinging the

tops of my ears and nose. I step into the snow, noting how my footprints from last night are completely covered. Retracing my steps, I note Heath's are gone too. Funny how easy it is to wipe away all traces of a person up here.

You're thinking of him again. A voice buffets my eardrums. I turn an ear toward the wind, hoping it will drown him out.

Though I stay under the overhang, the snow reaches my knees. Out in the yard, it's definitely deeper. I struggle through it and peer around the corner of the house and down the driveway. Snow blows in my eyes, making it difficult to see even as far as the front porch, much less down the hill to where the carriage house is. I rub the flakes from my lashes and reach for the firewood as someone steps out from behind the stack.

I scuttle backward, dropping the log, but catch my scream in my throat before it can erupt.

Heath.

"Hey!" he says brightly, reaching down and picking up the log for me. "Did I scare you?"

"No," I say, trying to be casual. "I just didn't expect you… So you didn't leave?"

He laughs. "What do you think?"

Stupid question, Seda. You're really brilliant.

"Mother Nature's either screwing us, or she wants us to get to know each other a little better. What do you think?" he continues.

I blush and look down at my feet. "I-I don't…"

"So, now's not a good time to…" He points toward the kitchen door, as I remember how I told him he might be able to sneak in and take some of our food.

I look back at the kitchen door. My mother is right inside. All she'd have to do is peek out the window over the sink, and she'd see him. I nudge him against the firewood pile, out of sight. "No. Not now. She's making breakfast in there. You've got to…"

"OK, OK," he says, trying to calm me. He must think my mother is some kind of Godzilla. "Relax. We're just…moments from cannibalism. And not just because we're hungry. Becca won't stop complaining. If we eat her first, maybe we'll finally have some peace and quiet."

That brings a smile to my face, but the smile is short-lived. My mom put pancakes on for me. They'll get cold, and if there's one thing my mom can't stand, it's me not eating food when it's hot and ready. If I spend any more time out here, she'll come looking for me. "I'll try to bring you something later," I mumble, but he's not paying attention. He's sniffing the air.

"Oh, hell. Are you eating…*pancakes*?"

The scent was heavy inside the house, but I can't really

detect it out here in the driving wind. But he's obviously caught a whiff, which makes sense. That hot dog he ate last night isn't going to cut it.

I push long, windblown strands of hair behind my ears and stutter, "I can try to…maybe…" I wonder how I could manage that. My mom definitely has our pancake batter rationed. Unlike with the hot dogs, she'll know if that's gone.

"So, this is a murder mystery house, huh?" he asks.

"Yeah," I tell him, glad he's changed the subject. "When we first came here, I got a fright a second, with all the creepy decorations lurking behind every corner."

"I don't doubt it," he says, thrusting his chin in the direction of the woodpile. I crane my neck to see. There's an empty spot where he must've removed some of the wood, and on the stone wall, in old, blackish rust, is a spray of what looks like dried blood.

The snow crunching behind me doesn't register until it's too late. I whirl around to see my mother standing there in her flannel nightgown and duck boots, staring at our new guest. I can't make out the expression on her face, but Sawyer fills in the blank.

You are in so much trouble. They're going to find out. And by then it'll be too late.

12

Stay for a night or the whole weekend. We have the vacation to suit your needs. We also host group team-building events, bachelor-bachelorette parties, weddings, bridal showers, retirement parties, birthday parties, and more! For an additional fee, we will customize one of our story lines to fit your needs. We guarantee a pulse-racing, hair-raising experience like no other!

MY mother is grinning her head off as she opens the front door, watching the onslaught of visitors make their way up the driveway to the snow-covered porch. I can't see them from my place behind the check-in desk, but I can hear their laughter. In my mind, they're throwing snowballs and the girls are shrieking and they're back to feeling invincible again.

"Mom," I mutter as another cold gust of wind blows through the foyer, tinkling the crystals in the dusty chandelier overhead. "What about the food?"

She's not looking at me. She has her fisherman sweater up to her ears and is shivering dramatically in the bracing cold. "Oh, we'll make do."

"What about…" My voice is quieter. "Are you sure this is a good idea?"

She turns to me. "Gosh, Seda, I don't know." She reaches over and massages my shoulder playfully. "You think it's a better idea to let them freeze on our front lawn?"

"But what if they—"

"Jeez, stop worrying so much, my little worrywart," she says surely. She pushes the door open wide and raises her voice an octave and singsongs as our guests approach. "Welcome! Welcome!"

Snow skitters across the worn welcome mat as they breeze in, thanking her breathlessly.

"Oh, of course!" My mother giggles as the five strangers filter into the foyer, carrying their backpacks and gear. They barrel over the welcome mat, and Heath is the only one who wipes his feet. They pile their belongings in the center of the hall, right at the foot of the old check-in desk. As they do, their eyes track wild circles around the place. Liam has the GoPro in his palm and is taking a panoramic shot.

My mom already has her arm around Becca, who leans into

her, taking the weight off her twisted ankle. They look comfortable standing together, like they're already the best of friends, even though they only met five minutes ago.

Becca gives me a little scowl. "I thought your mother didn't want us here," she says with an accusing lilt in her voice.

My mother looks at me, surprised. "What?" She shakes her head. "Oh, nonsense. Of course you can stay as long as you want. We have plenty of room. Lots of food too. It's warm and cozy in here."

"Oh God, tell me you have hot showers, and I'll never leave," Becca says, rubbing a kink from the back of her neck.

"Working on that," my mother says. "You really slept out in the carriage house all night?"

Despite being a victim of my shoddy brand of hospitality, Becca has managed to brush out her hair. It's not in two pigtails anymore. Now, the pink and blue ends curl prettily around her face. She pouts anyway. "It was so cold on that hard ground. I barely slept a wink, and I'm so sore."

My mother eats it up. She holds one of Becca's pale hands in hers. "Oh dear." She gives me a glare that sends a chill up my spine. "Seda. Go get more firewood, and let's get this place warmer. We usually only use the woodstove in the kitchen, but your hands are like ice!"

Heath puts a hand on my shoulder. "I've got this. How do I get to the woodpile from here?"

I point the way through the dining room and the kitchen, and he jogs out the back door, as my mother continues to pepper them with question after question about how they came to be here. My mother, the perfect hostess. Last night, the mood was darker, because they'd been on edge. Now they're all smiling and laughing, like they were in the store when I first met them. Invincible.

Heath returns a few moments later with a pile of firewood. I open the French doors to the giant living room, which has nothing in it but an old leather sofa and an oriental rug. We never use this room because the first day we got here, Zoe managed to lock herself in and we couldn't get her out for hours. Despite the room having the biggest fireplace on the first level, its walls are ripped to shreds, as if some wild animal got its claws into every last inch of the wallpaper.

Heath eyes those walls curiously as he sets the firewood on the hearth. "This is where the owner kept his dogs," I explain. "I mean, that was the story. As part of the murder house. When the owners died, the dogs were stuck in here and went crazy, clawing their way out. They managed to survive by eating the bodies of the victims. Or something."

"That's gruesome."

"But it's not real. It's likely my aunt and uncle slashed the wallpaper themselves to make the room spooky."

I hadn't noticed the rest of them following us into the room, so I nearly jump when Astrid says, "Wild!"

She seems entirely too excited by this place. In fact, they all do, minus Becca, whose complexion is still a little green. Liam drops his GoPro for a second and says, "So what else is in this house? I want a tour."

"Please tell me the whole house isn't full of stuff like this," Becca moans.

No, it's full of *much worse* stuff than this. I suck in a breath as thunder begins to roll in the distance. The sounds grows louder and louder until my four brothers and sisters appear on the upstairs landing, squeezing their chubby faces between the slats of the railings. "Hi!" Zoe shrieks. "Hi! Hi! Hi!"

They barrel down the stairs like a pack of monkeys, almost like it's Christmas and they have no idea which present to unwrap first. Their eyes jolt wildly from each guest to the next. Finally, Zoe runs up to Astrid and envelops her knees in a giant hug. "Hi!"

Astrid smiles stiffly. "Um. Hi."

She starts to topple a little, so I grab Zoe's arm and loosen her death grip. "Easy, Zo," I tell her. She pulls away reluctantly and stuffs her thumb in her mouth. "These are my siblings. Adam, Avery, Zoe, and Zain. Obviously, they're shy."

Our guests laugh but are decidedly less interested in my siblings than my siblings are in them. This is like a long-awaited party for the twins. You'd think we'd locked them in a dark closet for the past week with the way they cartwheel around the room, screaming and squealing. I grab Adam as he rounds past me, preparing for another lap, because I know if I can rein him in, the rest of them will usually follow. "Calm," I whisper to him, grabbing his book and giving him a little smack over the head with it.

He says, "What are these people here for?"

The other three don't stop. Over the din, Mom says, "They ran into car trouble down the street, so they're going to stay with us and ride out the storm."

Zoe throws herself on the floor at Astrid's feet, lifting her shirt to show everyone her belly button. "Car trouble? Did their car get all smashed up? Did anyone die?"

I let out a breath. Heath laughs. "Not yet, kid," he says, as I lift her to her feet by her armpits and pull down her shirt.

"Sorry," I mumble, not even really sure what I'm apologizing for. For everything. My family, this house, everything that's to come.

Becca lets out a hiss of a breath and pulls a cord out of her backpack. "You guys have electricity, right? So I can plug in my phone?"

"There's no reception up here," I remind her gently.

She looks at me like I'm a moron. "Right. But I can still charge my phone for whenever we get out of here and there is reception, right?"

"Oh. Right," I mumble. God, she hates me. The rest of them start to go through their backpacks, pulling out their own cords, and we spend the next few minutes looking for outlets, until every one of their phones is plugged in. I'm looking at them, thinking about mine—which has been tucked in my bedside table for months—when my mother rubs her hands together and says, "Well, let's go find a place to set all your things, and then I'll make you breakfast. We have plenty of bedrooms upstairs."

Heath says, "Thanks, Dr. Helm, but really, we don't want to trouble you. We can all stay in there." He points to the living room.

Becca groans and says under her breath, "That room is super creepy, Heath."

"Nonsense," my mother says, already hurrying up the steps. "Come on. All the bedrooms have cozy mattresses that'll be better than a floor. So many rooms that you might get a little lost and need to follow a trail of bread crumbs!"

The kids race up on my mom's heels, excited to show off their home to these strangers. Our visitors follow. I watch how curious they are, how interested. I think I was the same way the first time we came here. A lifetime ago. "Oh my God!" Astrid shrieks, picking up a candlestick that's shaped like a squatting gargoyle and laughing. "This place is just like I pictured it! It's totally a haunted house!"

The kids clap, getting obvious pleasure from her excitement. Zoe tugs on her jacket. "Come see my room! Come see my room!"

"Yeah, yeah!" The other three chortle.

"Easy," I mutter to them. "There's plenty of time."

My mother leads our visitors down the hallway. Even with the lighting overhead, this vast hallway could never be described as bright. It's all mahogany panels and dusty arches. Even though most of the doors are open to let the light filter through, the dismal grayness from the storm outside makes everything look even more ghastly.

"Would you look at this," Wit says, running a hand through his scrubby hair and squinting at one of the brass panels. "This room belonged to Jeffrey Leonard, a famous rock star of the

1970s who was electrocuted when his electric guitar was not properly grounded."

My stomach sinks.

"That's not a real person," Astrid declares. Then she looks at me. "Right?"

I shrug. "Probably not."

"I mean, it says he was famous," Astrid continues, crossing her arms. "But I've never heard of him. So it's fake, right?"

Wit pretends to whip his phone out of his pocket and snaps, "Well, let me look up his Wikipedia page."

"Oh, it's real." Every head swings to my mother, who laughs. "In a manner of speaking, that is. Nothing to be afraid of."

"Still," Becca says, visibly shivering and rubbing the tops of her arms as she scans the never-ending hallway. "Do all the rooms have plaques like this?"

"Yes," my mother says, lifting Zoe in her arms. "Just one of the many quirks of this grand old house!"

Becca grabs Heath's arm and presses close to his side. "These rooms are even creepier, and knowing the people who stayed in them died...I think we should sleep downstairs. The fireplace is there, so it'll be warm, and we can all be together." She looks up at him, big eyes pleading. Wit starts to make chicken noises.

Liam groans. "Wit snores like a freaking chainsaw."

"And your farts can make the dead rise from their graves," he counters.

Becca shoots them both a death stare.

"Fine," Liam mumbles. "But I got dibs on that big-ass leather sofa."

Wit punches him, then puts him in a headlock. Liam struggles away. The kids start to squeal again, and I see Avery trying to coyly nudge Astrid toward her bedroom.

"Are you sure?" my mother asks, shuffling Zoe to her other hip. "I mean, we have plenty of rooms with beds, and we can make all of them super cozy for you."

"We're good," Becca says flatly, grabbing Heath by the hand.

Heath doesn't look all that thrilled. He gives me an apologetic shrug and says, "Yeah. I mean, we don't want to cause any extra trouble for you guys."

"It's no trouble, no trouble at all," my mother says again. "But whatever will make you most comfortable."

Becca looks anything but comfortable. "Where's the bathroom? I'd love to pee somewhere other than in a hole I dug in the snow."

I point the way toward the bathroom, which is about

halfway down the opposite hallway, past the nursery. She takes a tentative step toward it, then stops, pulling on her parka.

Wit starts to make the chicken noises again. Becca coolly pretends to scratch the side of her face with her middle finger, directing it at him. Then she shrugs. "I don't really have to go right now," she announces.

My mother tsks. "Oh dear. I forgot. The pipes seem to be frozen in the bathroom. I meant to get a hair dryer. I think I read we can unfreeze them that way."

"You only have one bathroom in this place?" Becca says like it's an accusation. Heath elbows her.

"Just one working one, yes, out of twelve," my mother says apologetically. "It was all the six of us needed."

"Ohhhkay." Becca looks at her snow boots and mumbles, "This is a true house of horrors."

My parents used to entertain all the time when we lived in Boston, so this is my mother's element. Her composure never wavers. "Oh, come now. There are no horrors here. All you need is a good imagination. There are no ghosts here to speak of, right, dearests?"

I mumble a yes. The rest of the kids nod eagerly. Zoe grins broadly. "Ghosts would scare me. But this is just our home."

Becca considers this for a moment. She obviously doesn't

want to be outdone in the bravery department by a four-year-old. "OK. OK," she says, eyeing the dark hallway. She shoves her hands in the pockets of her jeans.

My mother grins after her. "Don't worry. You'll feel more settled when you've eaten. I'm going to make you all the best brunch you've ever had. My cooking is to die for!"

13

—

Three meals a day are served family style in the formal
dining room, around a large Chippendale dining table
imported from Europe in the 1700s. You'll need plenty
of energy while having the daylights scared out of you,
so be sure to enjoy some of Chef John's exotic cre-
ations! Our Prime Rib Fridays are a visitor favorite, so
they shouldn't be missed, and our sumptuous Sunday
brunch features a champagne toast for all survivors!

FOR the next hour, I help my mother get a massive pile of
pancakes ready while our visitors settle into the living room. It
jolts me whenever I hear one of them laugh. Sure, my siblings
laugh and squeal a lot, but it's not the same. And I'm on edge,
like one wrong step will send this house of cards crashing down
around us.

I'm crouching next to the giant buffet, trying to pull out the
china plates, when Heath's deep voice rings out behind me. "I
can set the table, if you want."

I nearly drop the entire stack of pretty white plates. I turn and place the pile on the white lace tablecloth. "Uh. Thanks."

"Wow, you guys sure know how to do it up. I mean, paper plates would be fine for us. And…" He touches the blush-colored linen napkins. "I feel like I'm at my dad's country club."

"My mom doesn't do paper plates. She tries to be green. You know, not creating waste and stuff. She keeps telling me that this is the way they used to do meals when this was a hotel."

He reaches across the table and draws the stack of napkins toward him. "S'all good. It's cool that she wants to try to preserve this place and make it what it once was."

He folds napkins and I set out the plates in silence. When I look up, his napkin is shaped like a long-necked bird. I'm impressed but not surprised. He strikes me as someone who does everything well. He sets the napkin on a plate and moves on to the next as I say, "I usually just fold them into rectangles."

"I learned this on a Mediterranean cruise," he explains.

"I've always wanted to go on a cruise. We're going to go on one, if we ever sell this place."

The corners of his mouth turn down. "I brought the average age on board down to, like, fifty. There was nothing for kids to do, so I got really good at shuffleboard and napkin folding."

"Oh."

"I know, I must sound like an ass, complaining about going on a cruise." He continues, not really sad, but matter-of-fact. "My parents are big travelers and have always been determined that I not interfere with their way of life. Thus, I've been in boarding schools since I was seven. So, it's cool that your mom cares about who you are now, not just the person you're going to be when you grow up."

I reach into the drawer to pull out the silverware, and one of the knives slips out of my hands, clattering to the floor.

"What's wrong? I mean, your mom is OK, right? She doesn't seem half as worried about having visitors as you thought she'd be."

I try to shrug casually. I can play this off, no problem. Maybe I can spare him, and he can leave here without really knowing what's underneath my skin. "Like I said, my mother is different. She's protective of us. She's always worried about us getting hurt. She sees danger in things that seem safe, and safety in things I'd think are dangerous, so I never can anticipate how she's going to…" I stop. "I should've known she'd be OK with you being here. She used to love entertaining people and having fun. In fact, she lives for it. It's hilarious, because I'm sure this old house is full of lead paint and faulty wiring and stuff, but she's not worried about *that*."

He laughs and inspects the cobwebbed ceiling. "Well, old places have a lot of charm. This one included. I have an aunt who lives in an historic place like this in West Virginia. My uncle wanted to move and buy a new house, but she said that all new construction is slapped together. They won't ever build places like this again, with this much detail and care and expertise, you know? It's cool. Everything's cool."

How many times is he going to say that everything is cool? Maybe he thinks I'm high-strung for no reason and he's trying to get me to chill out. Like that would ever happen. "I guess. I think seeing you guys here reminds me how much I miss my friends back home," I say, which is true, even if it isn't the reason I'm so on edge. "I haven't been in touch with any of them since we left home."

"Ah." That, he obviously understands. "You had a lot of friends?"

"No. Two, really. Juliet and Rachel."

"Boyfriend?"

I think of Evan. We didn't even hold hands, so I can't say that counts. I shake my head. "You guys have been friends a long time?"

"Wit and I, yeah. We're on the swim team together with Astrid, and Becca is Astrid's best friend. Becca and I went out freshman year."

"Oh, you all swim?" Figures. Whenever I think of water, I dream of drowning in it.

"No. Not Becca. And not Liam. Liam gets roped in because he's Astrid's brother and the one with the wheels, since only seniors can have cars on campus at Shady View, and we're all juniors. Liam's kind of his own person. Quiet. Even Astrid can't really figure him out. But he's cool, I guess."

"Oh. So you're all...sixteen?"

He nods slowly. "Liam is seventeen."

"You look older."

"Really?" He clears his throat and unfolds and refolds a crease in the napkin. "I guess boarding school ages you. You homeschool?"

I nod. "For now, until we get back to Boston. If we ever get back to Boston." I swallow the bile in my throat. "Is the room OK for you? I know it's a little drafty."

"Aw, yeah. Fantastic. It's better than the carriage house." He finishes folding the next napkin. This one looks like a candle. He presents it to me for my approval.

I nod as enthusiastically as I can manage. "Becca made a good choice, if she's afraid. I mean, she doesn't have to be, of course. But that's the Safe Room."

He looks up from a half-folded square. "What?"

"The Safe Room. If you get too creeped out, you can go in there as an escape. It locks from the inside so that nothing outside can get to you." I swallow. "From the murder mystery games, I mean."

His brow wrinkles. "Huh. Really? I was thinking, if it's the place to retreat, why does it look like someone destroyed it? Why doesn't it have pretty pillows and Xanax and soft drinks?"

"Oh." He does have a point. "I don't know, really."

"You know my morbid curiosity. Would you give me a tour of this place later tonight?"

My pulse quickens. He said *me*, not *us*. "You mean, just me and you?"

"Yeah. It has secret tunnels and stuff, right? I love the history of old buildings. In my aunt's house I found a secret tunnel that was used by the Underground Railroad."

"But what about Becca?" I blurt out.

He laughs. "It's not a date. It's a ghost tour, and you saw her. She'd probably pee her pants."

My face heats. I remember traveling the old halls, trying to find secrets and treasures. I didn't scare easily, but eventually it got too eerie, coming across remnants of the murder house. Even though I knew the props were not real, my mind started playing tricks on me, and the more bloody handprints I found, the more I started to think that maybe…they could be real. "I don't think my mom would—"

"Like you didn't think your mom would like us inside the house?"

I let out a low breath. "Listen. You don't want to go anywhere with me. I might…"

He's watching me, amused. Why is it that every warning I give him is amusing? "Turn into a werewolf?" he fills in, only frustrating me more.

I sigh, exasperated. "You don't understand."

He sets a newly folded napkin on a plate, crosses his arms, and leans against the wall. "Then tell me. I'm listening."

It's only when I set a knife on the table that I realize my hands are shaking. How can I possibly explain? He has no idea what he's dealing with. "I've been through this house. It's not—"

"Oh shit." Heath startles, then pulls a mannequin hand off one of the seats by its slender, ghostly forefinger. It's splattered in red paint.

"Avery," I mumble. "She likes to play tricks. Actually, all the kids do, but Avery's the worst. You'd think they'd be so scared, but it's almost like they're too young to understand. They watch horror movies like it's nothing. Even *Saw*. They're immune to fear. I guess anyone would be if…"

He grins. "Fantastic. No wonder you're so jumpy."

I cringe. Jumpy might as well be my middle name. I take a deep breath and change the conversation. "My mother wanted to do a scavenger hunt for the kids today, and I was going to help her."

"Scavenger hunt?" he asks. "That sounds cool. We can help."

* * *

I'm not sure whether my mom thought we were entertaining the entire New England Patriots football team or what, but holy cow, she made a lot of food. Piles of pancakes and a whole plate full of fresh fruit from Art's, so much that I can barely see Becca, sitting across from me. My mother has to realize that if we use all the syrup and pancake batter now, we're going to have to eat oatmeal until we can get to the store when the snow melts. But that's the way she was whenever she entertained friends in Boston. She went all out. She never does anything halfway.

I don't blame our guests for wolfing down the food like it's their last meal. After all, they're half starved. Zoe and Zain stare openmouthed at for at least the first few minutes before resuming their normal chaos—disappearing under the tablecloth and playing with people's socked feet, since all our guests shed their snow boots when they came in. Unimpressed, Adam has his nose in a book, and Avery is doing her best to be grown up and follow the conversation.

"Like I was telling them," Heath explains to my mom and me between shovels of food, "Funnel Mountain has their biggest party of the year on Halloween. I was there two years ago, and it was pretty great. So we made a plan back in September that we were going to go. It usually doesn't snow like this so early though."

Avery grins. "I'm going to be a red Power Ranger for Halloween."

My heart catches in my throat. We all look at each other. My mother, perched at the head of the table, starts to say gently, "Well, sweetie—" when Liam breaks in.

"Sorry, kid. Halloween was yesterday."

It's like the breaking of a dam. First there is a slow cracking and seeping, then complete and utter havoc. Tears gather in Avery's eyes, and by the time the others realize the bomb that's been dropped, she's sobbing uncontrollably.

"But, Mom!" she cries. "You never told us!"

Astrid's mouth is open. "You guys are seriously so out of it that you don't even know what day it is?"

"Honey," my mother says to Avery, still wearing that hostess smile of hers, now slightly tarnished.

Adam breaks in. "It's not fair," he grumbles. They may fight all the time, but he's as loyal as hell to his twin. "I thought we'd be back home for Halloween."

Finally. I thought the kids had forgotten Boston. I've only been trying to remind them about it for the past month. I should've known that the mention of Halloween would get their attention. After all, there are only three times of year in their mind: Halloween, Christmas, and everything else.

Now the Z twins are crying too. It's not the candy. No, my mom thinks all that stuff increases hyperactivity, so she usually has us donate it to our dentist, who ships it to the troops overseas. The twins love dressing up in costumes. Last year their elementary school did a big party and parade around the building, and I've never seen Zoe smile so big. My mother was class mom, so of course it was done right, with plenty of thrills and the best snack buffet you could imagine.

Heath reaches over and gives Avery's shoulder a squeeze. "Hey. There's always next year, right?"

Zain whines, "But I wanna party!" Snot drips down his face. "You said, Mom! You said we'd have a party when Seda—"

"That's enough!" My mother says, her voice louder, but still pleasant. She looks at him pointedly. Becca looks on, like she can't believe there are heathens on earth who live this way. Liam lets out a snort as if he finds this amusing. The twins' crying grows louder, but my mother's hostess facade doesn't crack. She pats Zain's white-blond mop when he collapses into her lap. "Come on, kids. We can have a party right here."

Zain looks up. "We can?"

"Sure," she says. I see the wheels turning in her head. "I was planning it anyway for Seda's birthday. I think it's a perfect way to pass a snowy evening, don't you?"

"But it's not Halloween," Adam says glumly. "You only dress up for Halloween."

"Who says? We can pretend today is Halloween. It will be fun!" She winks mischievously. "And scary. Do we want scary?"

"Yeah. Scary!" Zoe says. "Really, really scary!"

Becca and Astrid look at each other in silence, like my mother just invited them to go skinny-dipping in the frigid lake outside. I'm sure the last thing they want to do is party it up with a bunch of imps. But I have no doubt that despite our limited resources, my mother will not only pull it off, but make it an event to remember.

Heath says, "Hell, yeah! The scarier the better. We can do it."

She grins at him, then rubs her hands together and smiles at the rest of the doubters who are sitting around the table. "I was already going to do a scavenger hunt for Seda because she's been so glum lately. And because it's her birthday tomorrow."

I look at her, horrified. For me? Really? As if I get all my excitement from goofy scavenger hunts. Last I heard, I was just going along with it. "I thought it was for the kids."

She winks at me. "Surprise! It'll be for all of you. And I'll put together a menu for a great feast."

Zoe asks timidly, "Will we be able to eat the cake that you—"

"Of course we'll have cake! Seda"—she looks at me—"I need you to bring down that big trunk. The one we found in the attic with all those costumes in it."

I nod.

Becca grimaces. "Oh, just what I want to do, wear a moth-eaten, spider-infested old costume."

My mother says, "The costumes are optional, since I know some of you brought your own. But if you change your mind, you're welcome to switch."

Heath says, "I have all the good Halloween music on my iPhone. We can do 'Monster Mash' until we puke."

Becca blinks at him. "All right, all right. Fine. Woo. Let's party," she mutters in a monotone, whirling her finger in the air.

Wit slumps in his chair, skating the tip of his fork in figure eights through the leftover syrup on his empty plate. "Yeah, let's do it. Sounds like a total blast."

"Let's clear the table, crew," Heath orders his friends. "It's the least we can do for you, ma'am, after this great breakfast."

Heath sure knows how to butter up adults. My mother smiles at him, clearly impressed by his chivalry. In Boston, she never had a chance to meet Evan or any of the boys in my class. I always assumed she'd be against me dating. But this is enough to make me think that she might be OK with me having someone like Heath as my boyfriend.

Then I realize I'm getting way ahead of myself and want to give myself a good, swift kick in the backside.

Still, as we start to clear the table, my chest flutters whenever he holds the swinging door to the kitchen for me. When the table is clear, he assumes the role of dishwasher, so I grab a dish towel and dry. Meanwhile, the others are helping to straighten the room and chatting about how the snow looks even higher than twenty inches and is still not stopping. "That oven looks big enough to fit a huge turkey," Heath remarks, looking rather silly, arms buried up to the elbows in my mother's pink rubber gloves.

Becca is knotting her hair into one of those messy buns that still manage to look put together and stylish. She nudges him. "Oh my God. Are you hungry again after all that?"

Wit's studying the oven. He pulls the massive door down and peers inside. "Or a person."

"You just ensured I'll never eat again," Astrid mumbles, making a face.

Heath runs a sponge over a dish and says, "Yeah, our Donner party days are over. Those pancakes rocked. I could get used to eating like that."

I smile as he hands me a dish, then notice that behind him, the other boys have switched their attention elsewhere. "Is this a freezer?"

I swallow.

Liam says, "Holy hell. This place really is like the Overlook Hotel."

We all stare at him. He's been so quiet up until now.

"*The Shining*, remember? I mean, think about it. A man who lived here went crazy and wanted to chop his family into bits." He pulls on the handle of the freezer. At least it's locked. We're all just staring at him, so he finishes, "In the movie, she locks him in the freezer. Or a pantry. I forget which."

Heath nods and leans into me. "Liam is a horror movie fanatic. He's seen all of them."

"It was a pantry," I answer automatically.

Heath blinks at me in surprise.

"Oh, so you've seen it? The dad was a writer, and you said your mom is a writer," he continues. He pulls the handle again, and—*click, click, click*—it won't budge. Thank God. "And there was this thing about creepy twins. Coincidence? I think not."

"The twins in the movie were identical; our twins are obviously fraternal. And it's a freezer," I finally will myself to say, trying to be casual as I stack the plates on the counter. "*Not* a pantry."

Liam won't give it up. "Can we take a peek in—"

"No," I snap.

Everyone turns toward me. Never before has that chill from outside been so noticeable inside these walls. Liam steps away and shoves his hands into his pockets. They stare at me, surprise on their faces. A long silence stretches on. I try to telepathically transmit the words *I told you so* to Heath, because he's their unofficial leader and they listen to him. But he isn't even looking at me. He's looking at the freezer door.

I lighten my voice. "The kids like to play hide-and-seek. We don't want them thinking that's a place to hide."

That doesn't break the tension. It's only when my mother comes in, sees us standing stiff as statues, and says, "How goes it?" that Heath relaxes and everyone else follows suit. My mother puts an arm around Becca. "Come on, kids. Let's go have a little fun."

14

SOME OF OUR MOST POPULAR STORY LINES:

1. A Tinseltown Tragedy
2. Tara and Tommy's Tragic Wedding
3. A Rock-and-Roll Murder Mystery
4. Cabin Fever
5. A Gothic Horror Mystery
6. Southern Belles and Bombshells
7. Holiday Weekend Havoc

FUELED by maple-syrup energy and the promise of a party, my siblings drag our guests out of the kitchen and up to the second floor so they can behold their nursery. The girls seem less than excited, but they go along with it—Astrid because there's nothing better to do and Becca because she obviously can't stand to be alone in this house. Zoe tugs Astrid up the stairs by the chunky infinity scarf around her neck, nearly choking her. "Wait, you little nut bag!" Astrid shrieks as she climbs up after Zoe. "Yeesh."

My mother has the same wild look in her eyes she used to get in Boston whenever any of our birthdays rolled around. I like that look. It makes me smile, because no one knows how to throw a party like my mom. She's rummaging through boxes in the closet and has already announced that we're going to have a bloody scavenger hunt, whatever that means. "Prepare to have the living daylights scared out of you," she says.

Wit and Liam pull their coats from the pile of wet clothes they left in the foyer and quickly disappear to check out the backyard, leaving me alone with Heath.

"So," I tell him. "My mom's on a mission. I'd better get that trunk of costumes."

He lets out a surprised laugh, like he's amazed I actually know how to joke. He follows me up the stairs, practically at my heels, like a Labrador. I stop halfway up. "You don't have to come."

He smiles. "I want to."

I suck in a breath and glare back at him. "You *shouldn't* come."

The smile disappears from his face. I turn around and continue up, but a second later I feel his heavy steps at my heels. I whirl around. "Hello? Are you—"

"Not deaf. Stubborn. Tenacious." My scowl deepens, and

his grin becomes more angelic. "Come on. What am I going to do, sit in the foyer and count the ghosts? Let me help you. What, do you have a thing about having people in your bedroom?"

Not people. Just him. "It could be messy," I tell him.

We cross the landing and head down the dark back wing of the house. I know he is looking around at the walls the way I did when I first came here. This wing has no rooms and seemingly no purpose. It's just one long, narrow hall, the walls covered with rust-colored brocade. Every so often, there's a rectangular indentation underneath the wallpaper, where windows have been filled in. The only purpose of this hall, really, is for what's at the very end of it. It stops abruptly in shadow and looks like the deadest of dead ends. But off to the side, in an alcove, is my staircase. When we reach it, I start to climb the narrow spiral staircase, my footsteps clanging on the metal. He puts one foot on the bottom step and the whole thing sways, making me hold fast to the rusting handrail with both hands.

"Whoa. This thing safe?"

I shrug. As long as I've lived here, there have never been two people on this staircase.

When I get to the top, my eyes immediately fall on all the weird things I keep up here. At home, whenever Juliet or Rachel dropped by unexpectedly, all I had to worry about was maybe leaving a bra on the floor. Not that I ever had boys in my bedroom. I keep everything up here neat, but even though someone like Heath Hunter has probably been in dozens of girls' bedrooms, I'm sure he has never been in one like this. He stands frozen in the doorway, eyes wide. Handing this room over for inspection feels like handing over the key to my diary.

"This is your bedroom?" He sounds astonished.

I nod and start to tuck my hands into the back pockets of my jeans, then realize my duvet has a wrinkle. I reach over and flatten it out. "Weird, huh?"

He moves into the room so he's standing right underneath the rafter with the dangling mannequin parts. He touches a pink-polished toe. "Slightly."

It'll get weirder, the more details he notices, I'm sure. I step from one threadbare throw rug to the next, traversing rotting floorboards to the closet. My closet doesn't have a door. It's just a gash in the side of the wall between two crumbly brick chimneys where all my dresses (the ones I never wear anymore) are hung and all my shoes are neatly lined up in pairs on the wide floorboards. I pull Silly Sally off a rocker and toss her bloody form on the floor, then shove the rocker over toward the wall. Steadying it, I step onto the seat and reach for the shelf over my rack of clothes.

Heath is beside me in a second. "Whoa," he says. He's tall enough that he doesn't even need the rocker. He reaches for the heavy trunk and helps me lower it to the floor. Rather, I guide the box, but he manages the bulk of the weight without my help.

As the chest lands on the floor, dust puffs up around it. The box looks a little like a treasure chest, with a worn and curved lid as if it's been buried for centuries. The brass fixtures are a dull, scratched gray, and the latch is broken. Heath lifts the lid and pulls out a long, lavish red gown. "This one's mine," he deadpans, then bats his eyelashes suggestively as he holds it up to his body. "What do you think?"

He gets me so flustered that I can't think of anything to say in response. "My mother said they used to do theme nights," I explain in lieu of the witty comeback my mind won't formulate. "I think that one is from Hollywood night."

He raises an eyebrow. At least there's something he doesn't find creepy in here. We find some pin-striped suits, a gothic maid costume, a military uniform, a dress for a southern belle, and a crazy curly wig and shredded shirt for an eighties hair-band rock star. "These are awesome," he says, falling onto his backside and wiping the dust from his hands.

"Your Jason costume is OK though," I say.

"What, that? It's just a hockey mask."

"It's not going to be much of a party. I mean, my siblings—"

"It'll be sweet. You said your mom gets into it. Look, the least we can do is help those kids have a good Halloween after barging in on you guys," he announces, closing the top of the trunk. "And help you have a good birthday. How old are you going to be again?"

"Sixteen," I say. "Like you."

"Sweet sixteen, huh?" Now I feel all embarrassed again because he's studying my bed. "How do you sleep here?"

I let out a snort. "We should go downstairs now."

"What? Your mom doesn't want strange guys in your bedroom?"

That's the least of my worries. "We don't get many of those on this mountain, strange or otherwise."

He starts to pick up the trunk, then thinks better of it and slides it toward the staircase. "You really think you could've handled this trunk yourself? A little thing like you?"

No. But Sawyer could have helped me.

I wait for the throbbing in my stomach that usually accompanies every thought of my brother. But there's no throbbing, just a fluttering of excitement. Is this what people mean by butterflies? I've never had them. Sawyer has been very silent.

Maybe he's waiting. Or maybe the invincibility of our guests is starting to wear off on me.

I like that.

Suddenly, I like the idea of a party. It feels normal. "I'm strong," I tell him. "Feel my muscles."

I flex my bicep. He squeezes it, looking impressed. I'm flirting. I never thought it would come so naturally to me.

He wanders over toward my shelf, studying all the snow globes. He picks up the one with the Harvard Square scene and shakes it before losing interest and sliding it back in its place. Then he strolls over to my bed and sits. He bounces on the mattress once, twice, and the springs screech like a stuck pig. "Loud. And not very comfortable."

My heartbeat echoes in my ears. Without warning, he lifts up the pillow, where I keep my nightgown. "What are you doing?"

"Every girl I ever knew kept her secrets under her pillow." He seems upset that there's nothing there but my flannel nightshirt.

"I don't have secrets," I mumble, grabbing the pillow from him and setting it in place at the head of my bed. "Just a nightgown."

"Right." He bends forward and looks under the bed. My mind races. Before I can lunge and hold down the dust ruffle, he shouts a triumphant "Aha!"

And he pulls out a picture.

Act natural. "This your family?"

I nod. I won't look, not that it matters. Some memories are etched deep on my brain, like every pixel of that photo. If I looked, I'd see us all lined up, tallest to shortest, in front of the Christmas tree last year. We're all wearing matching green Christmas jammies with candy canes on them. Avery is making bunny ears behind Adam's head, and Zain is crying because he didn't get enough eggnog, but other than that, we look really, really happy.

My dad. My dad, who I haven't seen in...

My hands shake. I shove them in my back pocket. "Yes."

"Why're you hiding this picture under your bed?"

I open my mouth, but nothing comes out because I'm focused on the image of the man whose arm is tightly wrapped around my mom. He had floppy blond hair that fell in his face, and he was always tan, even in winter. Even though he'd lived in the United States since he was eighteen, he still had a very faint German accent. He always looked like he should be skiing the Alps. Of all the people in the family, he is the one who belonged up here in this snowy landscape the *most*.

He belonged here with us.

And he's gone.

"I get it," Heath murmurs sympathetically. "You can't even

talk to him. That's got to be hard. Even seeing his picture must be hard. You must miss him. But you'll see him soon, right?"

I realize my mouth is hanging open, so I clamp it shut before drool can fight its way over my bottom lip, then nod agreeably and in a conversation-ending way.

"Your mom's nice though," he says. "Really nice."

My mother always gets that kind of compliment. From the other kids at school, the parents, the letter carrier, who she'd leave hot cocoa and cookies for during the holidays. *Nice.* My mom, the woman who knows what to do or say in every situation. The woman who brightens a room just by walking into it. Of course Heath and the others have taken to her like they've known her their entire lives. She used to always come home late from the college because her students would line up for her office hours. Not for help with her class, but because she was a magnetic person they wanted to be around.

"So where's your twin?" Heath says casually.

On cue, my stomach roils, reminding me how far away from normal I am. "What?"

"Your siblings both have twins. Didn't you ever wonder whether you had one too?"

"I did, actually."

His eyes widen, urging me to continue.

"Not a real one. His name was Sawyer. When I was young, I used to talk to him." I'm blushing. I know this is totally bizarre. "But that was a long time ago. It wasn't until I was older that my mom told me that I had been part of a twin set, but I'd absorbed him in the womb. He's gone now. For a while, he was an imaginary friend, I guess."

"Really?" Heath grins, the opposite of what I thought he'd do, which is run away. "See, I knew there was more to you than met the eye, Seda Helm."

Suddenly, Zoe lets out one of her earsplitting shrieks, saving the day. I grab the brass picture frame from him and shove it back under my dust ruffle. "Let's go."

He stands up. "Yeah. Fine."

It's clear when I see the sick look on the girls' faces that my siblings have been up to their old tricks. Astrid practically runs out of the nursery, and Becca limps out after clutching the doorjamb and looking like she might throw up. "Stop it, you creatures!" she shrieks, stopping short when she sees Heath and me on the landing. She fixes a strand of blond hair behind her ear. "How can you live with these *monsters?*"

Zoe and Avery appear in the double doors, looking as innocent as two angels. "We didn't do anything," Avery sighs, picking at that scab on her elbow.

I close my eyes. I know what this is all about. I wag a finger at them. "Please tell me you didn't show them the intestines."

Zoe blinks. Avery looks at her feet. Oh no, they did.

Heath had been struggling with the weight of the costume chest. He drops it onto the runner and says, "Say what?"

I push past the girls and find Adam lying on the floor of the nursery, pretending to be disemboweled. Zain is in a corner, hysterical in tears from laughing so hard. I pull the boa of gore off Adam and mutter, "Cut it out."

When we first got here, one of the rooms had been made to look like a body had been completely chopped to bits. There was all this foam rubber made to look like guts, tied around a long string of intestines, coated in chunky red "flesh." The kids couldn't get enough of it. They wrapped the string around their bodies and paraded up and down the halls in it, like they were Miss America. Zoe sometimes slept wrapped up in it, like it was a blanket. Eventually though, it found its way to…somewhere. Probably under one of their beds. I should've known they'd whip it out for our guests. My siblings don't care about impressing anyone. They just want some reaction, good or bad.

The kids rush away, giggles echoing down the hall. I start to shove the guts under the bed when I realize Heath is in the doorway, laughing. "That is bizarre."

"Get used to it," I say under my breath. "You haven't seen anything yet."

He steps further into the nursery and looks carefully at each picture on the wall, Bambi and Thumper frolicking in the meadow, Bambi with a butterfly on his nose, Bambi curled next to his mom. He picks Golly up off Zoe's lace comforter and her body flops in half, kissing her toes. "This would give me nightmares."

Of all the things to give a person nightmares, a stupid doll is the least of them. I snort. "Are you not the horror movie type?"

He shakes his head. "Hate them."

"Good thing you didn't grow up in *my* family," I mutter.

"Oh my God!" someone shouts from the hallway.

We find Becca and Astrid standing around the trunk, but that's not what they're looking at. They're looking at one of Zoe's dolls, a Raggedy Andy with triangle eyes, unraveling yarn hair, and dirty overalls. Astrid picks up one floppy leg and shows it to Heath. "It says *Forever*."

"All the dolls say that," I explain. "We found them when we got here, and the kids liked them so much that they refused to throw them away."

Astrid's eyes widen. "So?" Heath asks.

"*So?*" Astrid says, disgusted. "Don't you get it?"

"Obviously we don't, genius," Heath mutters. "What?"

She exhales, annoyed. "Ever was the name of the little girl from the story we told at camp. The one whose father chopped her to bits. Before he went insane, he used to be a doting father who'd give his daughter a doll every year on her birthday. Don't you see? *For Ever.* These dolls belonged to the dead girl."

Becca lets out a shriek and glues herself to Heath's side as he rolls his eyes. "Come on. Like Seda said, the Dead Girl was just another one of the Murder House's story lines." He grabs Raggedy Andy from her and inspects the writing, then puts the doll in Zoe's waiting arms. Zoe doesn't care who it belonged to before, real or make-believe, alive or dead.

"I guess." Astrid looks vaguely disgusted. Zoe hugs Raggedy Andy close to her body. She reluctantly turns her attention to the trunk, kicking open the top. "These the costumes?"

Becca reaches in, pulls out the red dress, shakes it, and holds it against her body. She sways from side to side, modeling it. "Now *this* is a costume."

"That's mine," Heath repeats.

I'm pretty sure an hour ago the girls were firmly against the moldy, moth-eaten costumes. But I guess they've changed their tune, from the way Becca is eyeing the red dress like she can already see herself in it. "You can wear it," I tell her to be nice. She gives me a scowl, as if it already belongs to her. *OK…*

Astrid is on her hands and knees, sifting through the fabrics. She pulls out a flapper costume that's mostly a bunch of green tassels and tosses it at Heath. "You can wear this one. It'll show off your legs." She reaches deeper into the trunk. "Oh, yes, yes, yes!"

She pulls out the curly black wig. She shakes it out and grimaces. "It smells weird. But it's awesome."

Becca asks, "What is that supposed to be?"

She pulls out the ripped T-shirt and holds it up. "A freaking rock star. I love it. I can be, like, Slash from Guns N' Roses."

Becca wrinkles her nose. "Who?"

"What about you, then?" Heath asks. It takes me a moment before I realize he's talking to me.

"Oh, I wasn't—"

"Nonsense. Everyone here wears a costume, and that's an order…from your commanding officer. I'm going to be Robert E. Lee here," he drawls in a ridiculous southern accent, lifting up the old military costume. "And you can be my sweet southern belle."

I blush. I look over at Becca, who's shooting daggers at me with her eyes. I reach over and rifle through the pile of fabric for the maid costume, which looked enormous, but I'll make do. For some reason, I can't find it. "I…" They're all looking at me. I don't want them looking at me. I finally grab hold of the flapper costume and mumble, "I'll wear this one."

"Hey, you all! How are you making out?"

My mom stands at the entrance to the west wing, partially in shadows, holding a giant crate. Her cheeks are flushed in a way they haven't been since her summer sunburn faded, and she's breathing hard. Something in her eyes is slightly unfocused. She's excited, no doubt. Really, really excited about this, because she shivers a little, and that's when I see where the maid costume has gone. She's wearing it, of course, and it fits her perfectly.

"Other than your kids scaring the bejeezus out of us, fine," Becca mutters, throwing the red dress over the railing and pulling her hair out of its ponytail. It cascades perfectly over her shoulders, all shiny and golden, not a split end in sight. "I've had so many heart attacks since I got here that I'm surprised my heart is still beating."

My mother tsks. "They're super excited to have visitors. We love visitors. It's been so long. Too long."

"There's a shocker," Astrid mumbles under her breath, fixing the wig over her head. Then she calls sweetly, "Can we help you with anything, Dr. Helm?"

"Oh yes, I have jobs for all of you. But not just yet. Say-Say dear…" she says to me, inspecting the contents of her crate. From here, I can't see what's inside. "I think we might have some board games in the downstairs closet. You all can play there while I finish setting everything out for the scavenger hunt. I want it to be a real surprise."

I nod.

"You're going to love this. Just love this," she gushes before turning on her heel and heading down the hallway.

Astrid and Becca smile after her. My skin fountains with goose bumps. Whenever Mom gets to planning things, she goes a little crazy. Planning gets her high, but it's no fun when she's coming down. She absolutely hates the cleanup, so I'm usually in charge of that. I need to talk to her, reel in her expectations so that she doesn't crash when the fun's all over, or if it doesn't work out the way she wants it to.

Heath laughs. "You know what we're going to look like, right? A game of Clue. Colonel Mustard, Miss Scarlet…"

"Let's just hope nobody gets murdered," Astrid says, playing with the frayed white ends of her cape. "That would really suck."

15

Our hotel features an intense, frightening experience. Much of it is not suitable for children. Therefore, all guests must be ages eighteen and over. *No exceptions* will be made.

LOOKS like we're stuck on Fantasy Island.

The decision was between that and an equally ancient game of Scrabble with real wooden tiles, the only two games I managed to scrounge off the top shelf of the foyer closet. The closet is huge, so there might have been more, shoved deep in one of the cubbies among the old crocheted scarves and hats, but after finding the two, I put my hand on a fur stole made with entire bodies of rat-like creatures—beady eyes and all—and saw a snapped mouse-trap in the corner with the lumpy remains of *something* caught in its clutches, not to mention nearly overdosed on the stench of mothballs, so I decided the two games were good enough.

Liam and Wit blow in with a gale as I'm dusting off the

board games. They look like two survivors from a North Pole expedition gone awry, covered from head to toe in snow. Liam had heard about the cemetery from Heath, so they'd walked over there to take a look. But they hadn't gotten very far before they came upon the lake.

"It's wild," Liam says, addressing me for the first time ever. "We walked out on the ice, and did you know there are things under the water?"

"Like what?" Becca asks.

"Like clothing. And boxes. I saw an old license plate, I think. Might even be part of a whole car."

"Are you sure?" I ask, picking up their wet coats. "I never noticed that."

"We tried to cut through the ice, but we didn't have anything sharp enough," Wit says, shaking the icy pellets from his hair. "It's deep, that lake, huh?"

"I don't know," I answer dismissively. "I think. We keep the kids away from it because they can't swim."

"What are you talking about?" A voice cuts from upstairs. We all look to see my mother standing on the top landing. Before Wit can explain, she says, "Those things are likely part of the game, you know. On summer evenings they used to take the murder parties outdoors."

Becca hugs herself and mutters, "How romantic."

Mom claps her hands and shoos us off to the Safe Room. "Go on, have fun. I have to put the final touches on the hunt!"

I stoke up a warm fire for our polar explorers while they decide on a game. They pick Fantasy Island because it's the less academic of the two, even though none of them have actually ever seen the television show it was supposedly based on. I have no idea what my mother is planning, but whatever it is, she obviously doesn't want my help, so I sit down on the oriental rug to play. I barely say a word the entire time, though the rest of them get pretty into it. After we play twice (Becca wins both times) though, it starts to get old.

"I want to be the Princess now," Astrid says, trying to grab the card from Becca. "Give it up."

Becca lifts her bottom and triumphantly plants the card under her backside.

Wit says, "Looks like whoever wants to be Princess will have to pry it out from under her cold, dead butt." He scowls at her. "Which can be arranged. But I guess I'll be Starship Captain then."

Astrid tosses her Rock Star card across the room.

I've been the Detective both times, and though it was funny the first time, it was way less interesting the second, and I'm even less excited about playing a third time. As if she can read my mind, Astrid sighs. "I'm going insane. Can't we do something else?" She looks at me. "What's your mom doing anyway?"

I scoot to my feet, almost too eager. "I'll check."

The second I get out of the Safe Room, I let out the breath I'd been holding. But the feeling of relief ends when I see my mother struggling to pull a dead body down the stairs.

Every hair I have stands on end for that one split second, until I realize it's just the mannequin from my bedroom, Silly Sally.

The mannequin is dressed in the flapper costume. I help my mother take its feet, and we settle it on the floor of the foyer, right underneath the crystal chandelier. My mom reaches into her crate and pulls out a plastic bottle of fake blood. She starts to dribble it all over the body, getting some of it on the carpet runner. "Mom, you know—"

She smiles. "The more gore, the better. I think you told me that?"

I doubt anyone will be afraid of what is obviously a mannequin, but I feel bad telling her that. She always tries to make everything perfect for everyone. "Are you OK, Mom?"

She nods, spilling fake blood onto the pale body parts of the mannequin until it's coursing through her fingers and making black puddles underneath Sally. "It'll be good to use this stuff, rather than just throwing it away." She looks up suddenly. "And how are you? Are you having fun and making friends?"

"It's OK so far." My hands travel to my stomach. "The kids are nice."

She reaches out to touch my cheek, but I flinch because her hand is covered in sticky, red blood. She yanks it away. "I'm doing all this for you, really. I think you'll get a kick out of it. Everyone will."

"Thanks," I say. The mannequin's elbow is twisted oddly, so I push it down so that it looks more natural. Though dead doesn't necessarily look natural, does it? I throw a lock of the mannequin's long black hair over its pure white smile. "What is this for?"

As the words come out, my stomach twists. Sawyer is waking up after a long, long sleep, and he's not very happy.

No. No. I'm just hungry. *Shut up, shut up, shut up*, I repeat in my head to drown out his voice, even though it never comes.

Mom doesn't notice the way I clutch at my stomach. "It's my original murder mystery story. I spent all last night writing it. 'Who Killed Frieda the Flapper?' Great, huh?" When I don't answer, she says, "Are they all dressed in their costumes?"

The vibrations in my stomach are like a steady drumbeat.

Go away. I shake my head absently. "Not yet. Are you sure you want to…"

"Of course!" She smiles at me, and her eyes sweep over my messy ponytail. "Let's get you into a nice costume too. Take a shower and do your hair so we can celebrate, birthday girl. I unfroze the pipes and left the water running, so the bathroom's right as rain now. It'll be good to see how much life—or death—this old murder house has left. Right?"

She sweeps a lock of my hair away from my face. I flinch. I'm not sure. Not sure at all. From the way my stomach is somersaulting, one of us likes the idea. Maybe it's me. Maybe it's Sawyer. But anything Sawyer likes…scares me.

I squeeze my way into the Safe Room, where our guests are just finishing their third game.

"Time to get dressed. My mother wants you all in your costumes," I say. "The party is about to begin."

16

Feeling stressed? Some guests find the atmosphere to be more intense than they expected. Feel free to visit our Safe Room, located off the foyer. Read a book or magazine, and have some freshly brewed tea. The elements of the game will not to intrude there.

Remember, the name of the game is fun!

I SUPPOSE it's sunset, but it's hard to tell because there's no sun. The day has been entirely gray. Now it's a darker and more foreboding shade of gray. Grim daylight is the only light as I step to the railing above the foyer and look down over the scene. If it wasn't for Silly Sally lying in a pool of blood on the carpet, it would be just another night at this creepy old house. That… and four lanterns, glowing dimly atop the check-in desk.

My siblings are dressed like skeletons. They've outgrown their dress-up clothes, and the only outfits they could find on such short notice were their black long underwear. My mom painted glow-in-the-dark "bones" on them, and voilà! Even with black and white face paint, Avery looks vaguely annoyed she can't be a Power Ranger. I know she's going to be a pisser all night, even if this is a party. She pulls the hood of her shirt over her head, covering her wild mop of blond hair, and says, "Where's Mom?"

I look around. Sniff the air. Can't really discern any food smells, but she's got to be working on the feast. I hear a faint noise that could be either the clanking of our heating system or someone sifting through the pots in the cabinets downstairs. "Kitchen. She has a lot of cooking to do for dinner," I say.

Zoe tries to wrap her arms around me, but my giant hoop skirt gets in the way, so she slumps against it. "You look pretty, Say-Say."

I gnaw on my lip. Before my mom started rattling pans in the kitchen, she dried my hair, and it's shiny and light. I look prettier than I have in a while. I glance down at the glimpse of cleavage peeking from the top of my gown and shiver. I feel practically naked. I know Becca will think I'm trying to steal Heath from her and hate me even more, but whatever. My flapper idea went south the second Silly Sally became the murder victim. I grab my skirts and take the first of the steps as my skeleton siblings rush down the stairs around me.

"Wow, cool!" Adam shouts, pumping his fist when he sees the bloody mannequin. "Is this for us?"

The door to the Safe Room opens, and Becca appears. Her eyes fall on Silly Sally and she lets out an earsplitting scream, clutching Wit, who's unfortunate enough to be standing right next to her.

"Ow," Wit grumbles, pressing on his ear and shaking her off. "Chill."

She blushes and limps up to the grisly scene. "I thought it was real. What the hell?"

Even barefoot, she gives the red dress elegance, her curves filling it out in a way that would make most girls jealous. I instinctively cross my arms over my chest as she looks up and spies me. "Oh. Hi," she mumbles. "Nice dress."

I force a smile and then have the feeling I'm being watched. When I look up at the door, Heath's eyes are on me. I've barely had any conversations with any guy other than Evan, so I can't say I have a lot of information on the male mind. But I can tell right away that Heath likes what he sees. It's written in the rapt, openmouthed stare on his face. Evan was always so difficult to read; he usually looked bored or uninterested.

I watch Heath as he crosses the floor, being careful to step over Silly Sally. The general's jacket is too small for him, so he has it open, but the rest of the costume fits him perfectly, right up to the rakish cap atop his head. He stops at the foot of the stairs and reaches for my hand. When he takes it, he leans over and brushes his lips lightly over my knuckles. "Robert E. Lee, at your service, my lady."

I can't help but smile.

"Um. Dorkface," Wit pipes up. He's wearing a bow tie, suspenders, and thick black glasses from the trunk. "That's a World War Two general's uniform."

Heath doesn't stop smiling at me. "Screw off, Wit. Who are you supposed to be, a nerd? Not much of a costume." Before Wit can follow up with one of his witty retorts, Heath turns his back to him and offers me his elbow. "Shall we go solve a murder?"

I can't speak, can't move, can't breathe. It takes Zoe nudging me from behind to wake me up. I nod dumbly. "Y-yes."

Liam—at least I think it's Liam, since he's filming with the GoPro—is wearing that ugly mask again. He has on a tan vest and one of those white open-necked pirate's shirts. "So where's your mom? She going to emcee this, or what?" Then he starts to sweep his camera around the room and narrate in a low, dramatic voice: "Here we are as the mystery begins. There is a murder to solve, one that might be this house's last. The victim, lying dead on the carpet in the center of the foyer, appears to be a young Caucasian woman. There is a ton of blood, and a deranged murderer is on the loose in this very home."

The hoop skirt swooshes on the ground as I step off the bottom step and release the railing. The door to the dining room is closed, with only darkness in the space underneath. Taking a deep breath, I start to call out to my mother when I realize something is printed on a large white paper on the check-in desk. The first line says *Greetings* in my mother's handwriting. "Look at this," I say.

They all converge on where I am. Astrid practically has to climb over Zoe to get to the counter. She picks up a lantern and the paper and studies it, her eyes glowing in the orange lantern light. "Oh jeez."

Becca sighs dramatically and tosses her hair. "What? Just read it already."

Astrid clears her throat. "'Greetings, victims,'" she announces in a foreboding voice.

"Victims? This sounds horrible already." Becca takes a step backward, then realizes she's out of the small circle of light and reaches for Wit. Adam is between them though, so instead she ends up draping herself over Adam's head. He shakes her away, annoyed.

"No, it doesn't. It sounds wicked," Liam snaps at her through his mask. He gives his sister a thumbs-up. "Keep reading."

"'Who killed Frieda the Flapper? You have already been

broken into three groups, so before you leave… Are you team red, team yellow, or team blue? Look on your inside sleeve.'"

"Great. Verse," Becca mumbles.

We all look anyway. My dress is off-the-shoulder with layers of wispy, mint-green chiffon. I lift up one layer and see a tiny red heart sticker placed underneath the fabric. When did my mother manage this? I look up and see Heath holding a red heart sticker on the pad of his finger. Did my mother do that on purpose? The kids are each comparing stickers of the different colors—red hearts, yellow moons, blue stars.

"They're magically delicious," Wit mutters, holding up his blue star.

Becca reaches for Zoe, and for the first time, her voice is almost pleasant. "Hey. Little girl. Trade with me. I—"

"No, listen to this," Astrid announces. "'These teams were chosen with great care. Follow these rules, and your life we might spare.'"

Becca freezes. She scowls. She flicks her yellow moon off her finger with a long painted fingernail. "Brilliant." Her voice is back to normal. She glances at Liam as she pulls her feather boa up around her ears. "I guess you and I are teammates."

Liam groans. "Fantastic. Kill me now."

Astrid continues, "'The envelope will provide the first clue.

Make haste to the next. It will show you what to do. When you find all nine, you will need to use what you know. But hurry and don't go slow. Be brave, and do not give in to your fright. The first victim dies at midnight. Do not let it be you…'"

Silence fills the room. Astrid looks up from the paper. "That's it." She flips it over and squints. "Oh, except for this: 'Remember, the name of this game is to have some fun. If you're too scared, yell *Time-out!* And all is done.' See, Becca? No problem."

Becca sniffs. I think she is on the verge of yelling *Time-out* right now.

"Here," Wit says, picking up three colored envelopes from the counter. "I guess we each get one of these."

Becca shivers. "But what? We're going to separate? In this old house? And what does it mean, the first victim dies? I don't like this." She leans over and rubs her ankle. "And I can barely walk, much less go on a scavenger hunt through a bunch of dark hallways."

Astrid sighs. "Stop complaining, will you?" She sets down the paper and picks up the blue envelope, then motions Wit forward. She tears open the envelope with her teeth and pulls out the paper. They both look incredibly excited as they study its message. I shiver a little and hand Heath ours. The envelope is from Mom's stationery, and the stickers I recognize as belonging to Avery. I can't believe my mother has done all this. Actually, I can. She gets so wrapped up that she gets carried away, and reason goes by the wayside.

That's why we're still here and not back in Boston. If we just humor her, all will be fine.

Heath tears open the envelope, and we find a picture—or a portion of a picture?—that's so close up it's hard to tell what it is. It looks like skin. And...blood? What is this? I knew my mother had a flair for entertaining, but I never thought she'd actually be good at my aunt and uncle's business. Heath flips over the card. It says *Tennessee Williams*.

"OK," he says. "Makes perfect sense."

"I'm glad it does to you," I say doubtfully. I peer at Becca's, and while I can't make out the word, it's pretty evident the card says something else, which I suppose is meant to keep the teams away from each other as much as possible.

"What do you think it means, that the first victim dies at midnight?" Astrid wonders. "Because it's, like, dinnertime. I'm hungry."

"Stop complaining," Becca mimics at her, but her eyes are wide and I'm sure she wants to know as much as the rest of us do. "Let's just get this over with."

ALONE

That's when I start counting skeletons and realize that Zain is gone.

17

Should you need assistance at any time during the game,
call out *Time-out*, and a staff member will assist you.

ZAIN'S the youngest, even if it is by just eleven minutes, and he's always been the mama's boy. The rest of us were pretty torn up the morning we woke up and found out that my dad was gone. I remember Adam and Avery rushing from room to room, calling his name, thinking he was playing a game. But it's my mom who always plays games like that, not my dad. Sensing something was wrong, my mother ushered us all down to Art's so that she could use the phone to call Dad's cell, but it went straight to voicemail. But Zain? Maybe it's because he didn't understand, but he didn't even ask about Dad once. He clung even tighter to my mother, as if she might be the next one to go. What he didn't understand is that we are the center of my mother's life, not her writing, not her teaching. Without us, she has nothing. She will go to the ends of the earth to protect us.

"He's probably cooking with my mom," I say lightly, carving a path among the people as I sweep through in my monstrosity of a dress. That makes sense. After all, Zain has no patience whatsoever. Three minutes into the game, he'll be crying for Mommy and ruining the whole thing. It's better she keeps him in the kitchen with her.

I push on the door to the dining room, expecting it to swing open as usual, but it's only when I barrel into it with my forehead that I realize it's locked.

I rub the bump on my head, embarrassed mostly, but partly stunned. That door is never locked. I trace my finger along the brass keyhole, then stoop and try to peer inside. Totally pointless.

"Guess those rooms are off-limits?" Heath asks.

I stare at the door as if mere brainpower will open it, still trying to comprehend what's going on.

"Yeah. We'd better get started," Liam says.

Wit nods. "I'm sure he'll turn up. There're only so many places he can be, right?"

I nod reluctantly. There are a million places—secret passages, rooms, deserted hallways—where he could be hiding. But that's the thing about the younger twins. They have the vocal cords to wake the dead. If Zain was in trouble, the entire house would hear about it. Even if the house is so sprawling it muffles one's cries. And my mother wants to keep the mood spooky, I'm sure. It wouldn't be very scary with people barging in on her while she's cooking our Halloween feast. I nod more surely.

"This'll be a lot easier if we put some light on the subject," Wit says, spinning the switch for the chandelier overhead. I hear it click on, but nothing happens.

He scratches his chin. "Or...not." He looks at me. "Your mom is hard-core. Did she want us to do this in the dark?"

I shrug. The wiring's so messed up in this house that it never surprises me when a switch doesn't provide the expected result. "I guess that's what the lanterns are for?"

"All right. Let's go." Heath says, taking a lantern and starting up the stairs.

"Go? Go where?" Becca moans. "All we have is a freaking piece of paper that has some person's name on it. How does that help with anything?"

"It's a puzzle," Liam mutters, heading up the stairs in front of her. "You have to figure it out."

Becca looks at her paper and sighs. "He makes crappy snack food. Puzzle solved. Can we go eat now?"

Liam shoves Becca toward the staircase. "Up, before I wrap that boa around your neck and choke you with it."

The rest of us look at one another like we're waiting for

the ice to thaw. Finally, Adam races up the staircase after them, grabs the paper from Becca, and studies it. "I think I know where to go."

Avery gets that competitive glint in her eyes. She imitates her twin, inspecting the blue team paper, and though I doubt she can read it as well as Adam did, she rubs her hands. "I bet I know where to go for this."

Wit pumps his fist and says, "Hands in." Avery, Astrid, and Wit put their hands together in a huddle, and he does some stupid cheer to psych them up. "And….break! Let's get it!"

They rush off in a fury. Oh, Avery is on the right team for sure. I have to smile, seeing her so excited.

That leaves Zoe, Heath, and me. "I guess we should go upstairs then?" I ask.

Heath shrugs. "Unless you want to keep her"—he motions to the mannequin on the floor—"company."

I shake my head. My mom will pout at me all night if I don't at least try to take full advantage of the game she's laid out for us. I point the way up the staircase, and we get started on our quest.

"You're a hard girl to figure out, Seda Helm," Heath says, climbing up behind me.

I toss my carefully fixed ringlets over my shoulder and adjust the sleeve on my dress self-consciously. It's supposed to be off the shoulder, but it's uncomfortable, just the same. Maybe it's because parts of my body are exposed that I don't normally go around exposing. Or maybe it's because even though my back is turned, I know Heath's eyes are fastened on me. "What does that mean? No I'm not."

"You tell us you don't want me in the house, and yet you're glad I'm here. You tell me you didn't want me coming up to your bedroom, and yet you clearly couldn't bring down that trunk without my help. Are you seriously conflicted, or do you simply like talking in opposites?"

"I…" I drop my gaze to the floor. "Can we just play the game?"

At the top of the steps, I look down one hallway and see a lantern, so we go down a different hallway. Zoe, fearless, leads the way. This hallway is where my mom's bedroom is, and where we've been doing a lot of the renovation, so we know it better than the others. I can still hear Becca grumbling about her ankle and Wit singing some song about how much he loves walking in the pitch-black down a creepy hallway when we reach the first door. By the time Heath holds up his lantern to read the plaque, their voices have faded.

He reads, "'This room belonged to royalty. King Charles

Jacques visited here. Lacking other diversion, he ate himself to death one winter night.'" He looks at me, and though his face is half hidden in shadow, I know he's smirking from his tone of voice. "Cheery."

Without warning, his stomach grumbles, really loudly, almost enough to shake the walls. I look at Zoe, and we both laugh.

He says, "The sooner we solve the murder, the sooner we can eat, right? I'm starving."

Zoe does a cartwheel down the hall and grumbles that she's hungry too. She hasn't ever eaten willingly. I can tell from the way she's been wedging herself between us that she's taken a liking to Heath. She'd probably agree with anything he says.

I nod. "I'm sorry. I thought my mom would've fed us beforehand."

"Hey, it's OK. This is fun." He looks down at Zoe and smiles. "You think we should go in here?"

She shakes her head.

"OK. We go on." He holds the lantern in front of us, and we take a few steps down the dark hall. It's so eerily quiet that our footsteps fall leaden on the wooden floor. "I wonder what Tennessee Williams means?"

I shrug. "He was a writer, right?"

He nods. "I guess. *Cat on a Hot Tin Roof.*"

"*A Streetcar Named Desire.*"

"Right." He ponders this for a while. "I got nothing."

"Me neither," I admit, feeling guilty. I mean, she's my mom, so I should probably have some idea where these clues are coming from. But she's never mentioned Tennessee Williams to me before. Ever. She's a writer, yes, but I didn't even know she liked plays. I didn't think she was interested in any kind of drama where people don't get killed senselessly.

"I'm tired," Zoe pouts.

Well, no wonder. Things were so topsy-turvy today that the kids didn't want to take their naps. I'd thought the excitement of having guests over had them climbing the walls like monkeys, but maybe it was exhaustion. They always act a little nuts when they're overtired. I lift Zoe into my arms, and she slumps against me, sucking her thumb. "You want bed?"

She nods, her breathing already slow and rhythmic. I think she may almost be asleep. "Do you mind if I put her in her bed?" I ask Heath. "It'll only take a minute."

"Be my guest."

When we get back out to the landing by the staircase, there's no sign of the other teams. I cross to the double nursery doors and pull them open, wondering if I'll step on something laid out for my mother's crazy murder house game. But then I remember that this is the kids' sanctuary, and my mom protects them. She'd never do anything to scare them. I settle Zoe in, and she mumbles, "Intestines."

I pull the intestines from under the bed and wrap them around her. "Better?"

But she's already asleep. When I turn around, Heath is staring at me. He smiles in a wicked way. "So you get to show me around this house all alone after all."

Before I can reply, the clock downstairs starts to chime the hour.

I'm used to it, but Heath jumps. Then he grins and takes my hand. "Oh, come on. It's me. I'm harmless."

"Sure you are," I say, chewing on my lip. "You know, I don't think you're on a winning team. I bet the rest of your friends are already halfway to finishing the whole thing."

"Maybe." He holds the door open and lets me pass through, and then we head into another wing, one I haven't been in since we first got here and started exploring the place. We'd found a family of dead rats in one room, which put an end to all the exploring pretty quickly. I thought it was the one Astrid and Wit went into, but now it's totally dark. "I don't really care about winning. I'm not competitive like Wit and Astrid. They're beasts. I fully expect them to figure out the mystery in the next few minutes. Team Drama Queen though? They're probably in a heap, crying, in the Safe Room."

"I'm glad Avery is on Wit and Astrid's team then. She's competitive. And Adam wants to be an actor, so it seems like he's on the right team too. It's almost like my mother knew this. Funny, huh?"

He nods. "Well, if we've got Team Drama Queen and Team Competitive, what does that make us?" He grins. "Team No Chance in Hell of Winning?"

I laugh. "No. I just didn't want to disappoint you. You seem competitive too."

He pauses. "Nah. I mean, I do?"

"Yeah. Well, you're on the swim team. And you said you ran a marathon last year."

I'm glad it's dark to hide the blush in my face that results when he looks at me, surprised. It must be obvious I've been hanging on his every word, trying to figure him out.

"Oh right. But I'm not really," he says. He lifts the lantern to read another plaque detailing another gruesome death. "I can't believe you live in this place. Not much scares me, but Becca has a point."

"I know, it's creepy. But my mother loves it here. It's hard to believe that six months ago she was just going to sell it. She saw it, and suddenly her entire life in Boston didn't matter anymore. When she's passionate about something, nothing can get in her way."

"And you? What are you passionate about?" When I look at him, he continues. "If you don't care about winning, what do you care about?"

I shrug. What I care about is that I am having fun with a normal guy my age. This is pretty close to heaven. Winning isn't necessary. "So what? You want to give up?"

"No. No, of course not," he says. "We must accept the challenge of today so we can feel the exhilaration of victory!"

I stare at him.

"Patton," he explains. "I did an oral report on him last year in my American history class. When I was a sophomore."

"Oh."

He grins. "But seriously, Wit's got this in the bag. And I'm having fun. Aren't you?"

I nod. If only he knew how much fun he was making my day—my life—he'd think I was really crazy.

"So, onward." He walks a little further. "Say something. You're too quiet. It's freaking me out. Even more than this creepy hallway."

"Uh. What do you want me to—"

"I know. Let's play a game. I'll ask you a question about something starting with an *A*, then you can ask me something starting with *B*, and we'll keep going." When I don't say anything, he adds, "Trust me. It's fun. We did it in orientation at Shady View."

"All right. You start."

He shifts the lantern into his other hand and rubs his chin. "*A*. Favorite letter of the alphabet?"

"*Y*," I say immediately.

"*Y*?" He ponders this. "Why?"

"See?" I laugh. "Because it's also a question. And it's a chameleon. It's a consonant, and sometimes a vowel."

"That's interesting. Me, I'm a fan of *X*. Not because of X-rated things, but because it marks the spot to buried treasure. But *W* is high on my list. It's a letter with a word in it. Double. I find that extraordinary. But it actually should have been called double *V*, if you think about it." He's babbling, and it's cute so I laugh some more. "OK, OK. Your turn."

"Favorite book?"

"Good!" he says, and I can tell he's impressed that I've taken to his game. Truthfully, I'm happy to be playing it, unlike the hundreds of games my mom makes to entertain the little kids. The dread that I usually feel while walking these hallways is gone. Even though it's pitch-black, everything seems a bit brighter. "*The Lion, the Witch and the Wardrobe.*"

"I love that book!" I blurt out, embarrassed because when have I ever felt so enthusiastic about anything? My mother has passion for movies, for entertaining, and for taking care of her kids, but I've never felt super excited about anything. I wonder if this is what passion feels like.

"Seriously though. I used to hide in my mother's armoire—she used to have a lot of furs—and wish the back would open up into a snowy forest. I always felt sad when all I found was a piece of wood."

"Right?" I say. "I wanted a friend like Mr. Tumnus."

"And I had no idea what Turkish Delight was, but I knew I wanted some."

Now we're laughing so much, and I'm sure if these walls were alive they'd be whispering in wonder about what we're doing, because have they ever heard laughter? All the plaques do is speak of death and sorrow. We've passed a couple more rooms without even looking at the placards, and now we're in an off-shoot of one of the wings, a narrow little hallway that looks like a dead end, with a creepy portrait of an old man in a white wig and a high, frilly collar from the colonial days.

"Well, hello, Dorian Gray," Heath says, making me laugh

so hard I start to clamp my hand over my mouth until I remember what he said about my smile. I fasten my hand at my side. The game continues. I tell him my favorite card game is crazy eights, I find out his favorite day of the week is Saturday, of course, and when he asks me how I like my eggs, I tell him I really don't like eggs.

"This is sad news," he says like it's the end of the world.

"Why?" I ask, confused.

"Eggs have protein."

"And cholesterol," I say, slapping his shoulder. "OK. My turn. What is the most fun you've ever had?"

"Truthfully?" We've stopped at the dead end, where there's a spindly little table underneath Dorian Gray's piercing stare. Heath sets the lantern down and leans against the wall, making himself comfortable. I lean against the wall opposite his. "Here. Now."

I blush. It's the most fun I've ever had, hands down. But with all the life experiences he's had, the cruises he's been on and places he's been and things he's seen… His face is partially shadowed, but there isn't a trace of insincerity on it. Maybe what he's saying is a line. Or maybe we just…click. I've heard stories about that, about kindred souls. Maybe that's what we are, maybe that accident was destiny. It almost seems too perfect to be real, that a boy my age could show up right when I needed him most… "Really?"

"Yeah. What can be better than touring an old house on a snowy evening with a beautiful southern belle? I feel like… You ever do that? When you're in a place and everything's perfect, and even in that very moment, you're positive that it's something you're going to remember for the rest of your life? This… I'll remember this forever."

I look down at the floor, because I think that I'm starting to cry. I never knew I was someone who could shed happy tears, that I could be emotional about a moment like this. Maybe it's because I'm thinking of everything I've lost. Maybe I'm simply overtired. "I'm having fun too," I say, wiping a tear from my eye.

"Hey, what's that all about?"

I sniff deeply, swipe at a few more tears, and shake my head. "Nothing. It's…" What can I say that will make sense to him without making me look pathetic? "It gets really lonely here sometimes."

OK, that's pathetic. I blink furiously to get rid of the tears, steeling myself.

"I get it. I want to write to you," he says. Now the murder hunt is a million miles from my mind. "I mean, I know I can't call you. But I can write you, right? Like, a letter?"

I've never written many letters, except for thank-you notes to family members who sent me birthday presents when I was a kid. I'd read about pen pals, and I even thought I might be able to do that with Rachel and Juliet, but I found some goofy cat postcards at Art's and sent them off to them earlier in the summer. I never got anything back.

"We have a PO box. But the post office is down at Art's. I'm not sure when we'll get back there. I mean, we're supposed to be leaving and going back to Boston. But Mom keeps saying that, and it never happens." Before he can put on the brakes, I quickly add, "But I'd really like that."

A slow smile spreads on his face, as if some great idea is occurring to him. "What letter were we on? *K*?"

I shake my head. "No, we were on—"

"When was the last time you were properly kissed?"

I raise an eyebrow, sure my cheeks are about to burst into flames. "We were on *G*."

"Don't avoid the question."

"I'm not avoiding it. You're breaking the rules of the game," I insist indignantly, putting my hands on my hips. Because I sure as hell am avoiding the question. "Besides, what kind of question is that? What does being *properly kissed* even mean?"

"Face it. There are a lot of ways to be kissed, and most of

them, sadly, are missing heat, chemistry. Or they have too much slobber, too many teeth. Am I right?"

"I don't know." I take a deep breath. I never would've been able to admit this to Evan, but the words come out so easily around Heath. "I'm sure mine would be lacking in a lot of things. I've never been kissed at all."

Now it's his turn to look surprised.

"But if you think you're breaking the rules of this game because you want to kiss me, you're mistaken," I quickly add, looking away.

"Am I? Damn. This is a worse ass-kicking than I got at Appomattox Courthouse."

I can't help but laugh. "You'll get over it, I'm sure."

He shakes his head, and the next time he speaks, he's entirely serious. "Nah."

In that moment, I can see that he's hurt. Not playacting hurt. I can see that he really wanted to kiss me. I let out a shaky breath. "We just met."

He holds out a finger. "But I feel like I've known you for a lot longer. Don't you feel the same way?"

Yes. Weirdly, yes. As cheesy as it sounds, it's true. "OK. Maybe…one kiss."

He doesn't have to be asked twice. He steps across the

hallway, taking my hand. He's gazing right at my lips when I suddenly feel cold, despite the heat in my face.

"That doesn't scare you away?" I murmur. "That I've never kissed anyone?"

What am I talking about? Of course it doesn't. He had a thousand other reasons to be scared of me. He's here now, despite my weirdness. Maybe even because of it. He's so close that I can feel his breath, fanning my cheek. He puts a finger underneath my chin, tilting my head up. "You OK with this?"

I've never been more OK with anything. Maybe I should be worried that my kiss won't be good, but I'm not. I'm comfortable. I want this. "Are you?"

"Hell yes, I want your mouth, adorable braces and all, on mine."

I close my eyes, and the next thing I feel are his lips, warm and soft, on mine. His tongue gently touches my lips, waiting for an invitation, so I open my mouth and let him in deeper. Not because I know what I'm doing, but because this all feels so natural, so right. When he stops kissing me, he whispers into my ear, "Now *that* was a proper kiss, I think."

"I'm not sure," I say with a shrug, smiling. "I have no point of comparison. But I think it was pretty good."

Understatement of the century. My knees are shaking, but

it doesn't matter because I might as well be floating. Can it really be that yesterday I felt like my life was ending? And then this perfect guy shows up, out of nowhere, with his fake plastic ax and his…

I freeze as my eyes trail to his hairline. "How is your forehead?"

"What?" He touches it.

It had seemed like a pretty big gash, enough to drip blood. He'd worn a square bandage over it until he changed into the costume. "It stopped bleeding."

"Oh yeah, last night," he says with a smile. "It was like a paper cut. You know? Bleeds like a mother but is actually really small. Which is great. It should heal fast. Although, maybe a scar would've made me look tough."

I shrug. "I like scars."

"Damn."

I squint. I can't see the cut in his hairline. There are too many shadows. "But you look good enough without one."

"You're a suspicious thing, aren't you?" he says, teasing me. He's looking at my lips, like he wants to kiss me again.

As much as I want it…suddenly, my stomach is roiling as if Sawyer's there, right on the other side of the next wave. "I have to use the bathroom," I say quickly.

He looks confused. "OK. You take the lantern. I'll wait here."

"In the dark? Are you sure?"

He nods. "Do I have any other choice? I'll try to come up with an idea about our clue."

I rush down the hallway and into our one good bathroom. Taking a deep breath, I hold up the lantern and look at myself in the mirror. The threat of doppelgängers doesn't scare me anymore. I'm a completely different person than I was, even earlier today. My hair is shiny, and although I can't see much in this small triangle of glass, I no longer look as pale as death. I look flushed…happy.

Clutching the edge of the sink, thinking of his mouth on mine, I run cold water and pat it on the back of my neck, trying to cool my feverishly hot skin. Then, out of the corner of my eye, I notice three envelopes—red, yellow, and blue—on the window ledge.

Whoops. I'm not sure I was supposed to run across these yet. My mother would probably be upset if I take the red one.

My eyes sweep the room, finally settling on the claw-foot tub where I took a shower only a couple of hours ago. I'd stepped out feeling confident, hardly able to believe that the last time I'd been in that tub, I'd held my breath under the pink-tinted water, wishing someone would hold me there. Back then, I'd been so hopeless. And now…for the first time, I think life might actually be OK.

My mother has drawn the shower curtain around the tub, and I'm sure she's probably put a ghastly mannequin behind there. I don't even bother to look. I run my fingers over my lips and wonder if they're too chapped. I can probably make it to my bedroom and back in a couple minutes. I step outside and crane my head down the winding hallway, but I can't see where I left Heath. I rush down the narrow hall to the dead end and climb up to my room. Then I apply my strawberry lip gloss. Funny, I haven't even worn it since June. I'd never cared.

As I'm hurrying back down the hallway toward Heath, a sound echoes from far behind me. It sounds like a screeching. Or even a scream.

I reach Heath as the scream fades.

"Did you—" He stops, because the sound comes again. It's a voice, definitely. All I make out is a long, stretched-out sound of alarm. *I'm…* Or maybe not. I can't be sure I heard right.

"*I'm?*" I repeat. "*I'm* what?"

"That's Liam," Heath says breathlessly. He lets out a nervous laugh. "He's probably trying to psych us out."

But I could've sworn he'd been screaming. And that he said "I'm" before getting cut off.

But maybe he was just calling for time-out.

18

Check-in is at 4:30 p.m. Friday or Saturday afternoon. If you arrive earlier, we will make every effort to have your room ready.

Checkout is promptly at 11:00 a.m. on Sunday (or as noted on holiday weekends). Should you not check out on time, a staff member will be along to make sure you are still among the living. A $40 late-checkout fee may apply.

EVERY hair on the back of my neck stands on end. I should be used to loud noises; after all, my siblings aren't exactly quiet. The sound doesn't sound like them though. It's lower—and definitely male.

Heath doesn't seem particularly worried. "You don't know Liam. He's probably sick of Becca's whining and wants to get out of the game. He's"—he lowers his voice and wraps his hand around mine—"kind of an a-hole."

"I thought he was your friend."

"We're not, really. Like I said, he has the wheels. But he doesn't have a whole lot of friends of his own. I mean, why else would a senior spend all his time with juniors? He's a moody bastard. He films everything and thinks he's going to be Wes Craven or something. Sometimes he's a regular guy, and sometimes he can turn on you and start screaming his head off for no reason. Astrid says he once pulled a knife on their dad."

My eyes widen.

"She told me once that he scared her."

"Scared her? How?" I swallow, thinking of Adam, who's sweet and timid and the exact opposite of that.

He shrugs. Now I'm really worried for my brother. I'm about to tell Heath that when I hear a single loud pop. We look at each other. "Was that a—"

"Sounded like a gunshot."

That doesn't do anything to settle my nerves. "Maybe we should go…"

He nods. "Yeah. Let's check it out."

We head purposefully down the hall toward the foyer. When we're nearly there, a dark figure steps out of the bathroom, sweeping across the hallway not twenty feet ahead of us. My heart lodges in my throat. We both jump back. I stifle a yelp with my palm, then let out a sigh of relief.

It's Liam, wearing a dark cape but the same grisly mask with the black, hollow eyes and long, gnarled nose. He turns to us and takes a step backward, suggesting he's as surprised to see us as we are to see him. "Yo, man." Heath salutes him. "What happened to your other costume?"

"Smelled like shit," he grumbles.

"Asshole," Heath mutters under his breath. He nudges me. "See, the jerk wanted a time-out so he could use the can."

"Where are Adam and Becca?" I call down the hallway.

He points over the railing, downstairs. "We're killing it." He chortles, his voice muffled by the mask. "We're going to wipe the floor with your asses, girls."

Heath lets out a breath. "Have fun with that," he calls jovially, then mutters, "you psycho." He looks at me and squeezes my hand. "See? Moody bastard."

When we reach the place where the hallway opens up to a balcony overlooking the foyer, I peer over the railing as Liam continues downstairs. Silly Sally's still lying there, her dead eyes staring up at the darkened chandelier. When he reaches the bottom step, Liam stalks across the hallway and disappears into one of the lower hallways. I'm about to call down to Adam when suddenly Heath says, "Hey, listen to this."

I turn and look at him. He's studying a plaque on the opposite wall.

"'This room belonged to Lionel Bellows, a World War II general who is thought to have been poisoned by enemies after a car accident left him incapacitated.'"

So Heath is back to playing the game now. His competitive side seems to be taking over after Liam's taunts. "So?"

"That sounds like..." Now the wheels in his head are really turning. "I mean, I did a report on it. That sounds like how Patton died."

I blink. I knew the plaques held crazy stories, but it never occurred to me that they could have some basis in reality. "Coincidence."

"Well, don't you get it?" he says. "That's what your mom was telling us. We asked if they were real, and do you remember what she said? She said *in a manner of speaking*. Because they *are* real, but they happened to different people. *Real people*. And maybe we need to match the dead celebrity on our card with the way they died."

He's breathing hard now, excited. I stare at him. It makes sense. "All right. But if it is true, we don't know how Tennessee Williams died, do we?"

"Suicide, right? I think." He thinks some more. "No, wait.

Wasn't he the one who choked on the bottle cap for his eye drops? At least, that was the story I remember from English class. Or was that Truman Capote?"

My breath catches. "Eye drops?" I clap my hands together. "There's a room with a plaque like that. I know where it is. Come on."

He grins, satisfied with himself, and follows me.

"We can win this, you know," Heath says as I lead him down the hallway to the Blue Room. "Astrid and Wit may be super competitive, but we're smarter. They'd never guess that."

"I thought you're not competitive," I say, my hands trembling as I think about kissing him. I can barely breathe. I can still feel the pressure of his lips on mine, how warm they were, how blissful and sweet he'd managed to make these gloomy halls.

"I'm not. Not completely. But Wit always loves one-upping me. I'd love to one-up him for once."

We stop at my mother's screening room. Heath reads the plaque out loud: "'The Blue Room belonged to playwright Edgar Wise. He choked to death in 1950 on a bottle cap for his eye drops.'" He pumps his fist and lets out a loud whoop. "Bingo!"

He pushes open the door, and we step into the room.

Heath lifts the lantern and arcs it back and forth, illuminating the hulking projector and the screen on the far wall. Then he freezes. "Look at that."

I peer around his husky form and see a shapeless lump on the floor. Heath lowers the lantern, and I can make out stiff mannequin hands, pale-white skin, and that forever stare. It's creepy but undoubtedly staged, which makes it less scary. The male mannequin is sprawled out on the ground, dressed in a dark suit. Heath brings the lantern closer and crouches beside it. Then he lifts a little bottle and passes it to me. It's a tiny bottle, like eye drops.

"So what does this mean?" I ask.

Heath looks around the room, but the lantern only illuminates the small circle we're in. The corners of the room are so dark that a person could be hiding there, and we'd never see them. Heath stretches his arm out with the lantern, spreading the meager glow of light onto the lumpy sofa.

There's a silver tray in the very center, topped with a pyramid of brownies, and beside it, a pile of napkins and a pitcher of milk. My mouth starts to water as I realize how hungry I am.

"Ha!" Heath says, dropping the lantern to his side and lunging for the tray. He picks up a brownie and holds it like a precious, delicate treasure. Then he hands it to me. "I knew your mom wouldn't starve us."

I smile. My mother does think of everything. I inhale the chocolaty goodness, then break off a piece and pop it in my mouth as Heath shoves an entire square into his. My mother makes the best brownies. He grins and takes two more.

"Hey!" I nudge him. "Don't you want to leave some for the others?"

He scoffs at the suggestion, wraps the brownies hastily in a napkin, and pockets them. "Your mom probably left food in all the rooms. Their fault for not getting the one with these awesome brownies first, right?"

I look around the room, toward the dresser with the small console that holds the last remaining shards of a mirror. Those last few pieces reflect the lantern, shining a bare light on the surface of the dresser.

Atop it are three envelopes: red, yellow, blue.

I lift my skirts and step over the mannequin, then reach to pick up the red envelope. I wave it in the air and open it. "Clue number two," I announce, motioning for Heath to bring the light forward. The picture is only part of a picture. It looks like someone's cheek, or maybe a hip? I'm not sure. Heath produces the first paper, and we try to fit them together. It's obvious they're part of the same puzzle, but they don't fit together. I sigh and turn the picture over, then read the name printed there. A chill creeps up my spine.

Heath lets out a long sigh. "Well, I'm at a loss. Who's that?"

I say, "Isadora Duncan. She was a famous dancer in the 1920s."

"OK," he says, still chewing. "Good. Do you happen to know how she—"

"Yes," I tell him. "Rumors say she was strangled and nearly decapitated."

19

Choose your room! Choose your persona! Would you like to be the brave general whose last meal was to die for? The playwright who had it all but "choked"? The rock star whose last show was truly "electrifying"? Or maybe you'd like to be the actor whose one shot at fame went straight to his head? It's up to you! We'll even provide the costume, in case you'd really like to get into your character!

"WAIT. Decapitated?" Heath shoves aside the tray and sits down on the couch. "Seriously?"

I nod. "She had on a long scarf, and she went for a ride in a convertible. It got caught in the spokes of the wheel and yanked her out of the car. Some people say she was choked so thoroughly that she was nearly decapitated."

"That's...grisly." He grimaces. My mom *did* say she was going with the gore. "So? You know of any rooms with plaques like that?"

"Yes. Down on the first floor. There's a parlor down there that could have something to do with it."

Heath grins at me. "I'm so glad I have you on my team. You're my ace in the hole."

I blush. "You're the one who made the connections that led us to this room."

When we step out into the hallway, Heath stops short and I nearly run nose-first into his shoulder blades. "Yo!" he calls. I step aside in time to see something move near the staircase at the end of the hallway.

"Who was that?"

"Liam, I think. What the hell is he up to?" We pick up the pace, rushing to the top of the steps. We peer over the railing, but once again, it's only Silly Sally. Nothing has changed. "Come on."

I follow Heath down the stairs. At the bottom of the steps, he stops and glances back at me. Even in the darkness I can see there's something wrong. He shifts back and forth on his feet. "Do you feel that?"

"Feel what?"

I actually hear it before I feel it. A squicky noise that someone would make if they were walking on a couple of wet sponges.

"Squishy." Heath bends down, touches the carpet, and brings his fingers into the light. They glisten with red. Blood. He sniffs it. "I guess your mom spilled some extra?"

I shrug. "I guess." I think of my mother, carrying that crate with the gallons of fake blood down the staircase. "She might not have realized she spilled some after setting up the mannequin. It's so dark in here."

"It's fake. At least, I hope." He grins.

He shines the lantern at our knees as we descend the hallway. Sure enough, there are several spatters of blood dampening the carpet, like a trail. I know Mom was planning to replace these carpets, so it's not a big deal. But I wonder if the kids are at all frightened by any of this.

The kids. Have they ever been this quiet? Zoe is asleep, and she's the shrieker. Zain is with Mom, and with the door to the kitchen closed, I probably wouldn't be able to hear him anyway. Avery and Adam…well, they're a little less excitable. Still, guilt blooms in the pit of my stomach. I was so busy advancing my love life with Heath that I completely forgot about my siblings. "I should probably check on the kids," I tell Heath. "Adam? Avery?" I call.

No response. The only noise is the ticking of the grandfather clock.

"They could be anywhere," I say. "They don't always come when I call them."

"Yeah, didn't you say you could scream bloody murder at one end of the house, and no one at the other end could hear it?"

I nod.

He motions me to the check-in desk. Then he points down the nearest hall and raises an eyebrow. I nod. We follow it. I think this was the hall that Astrid's team went down, but it appears to be empty. Heath slows at a set of double doors on the left and reads the plaque. "'Swimming Pool. Several guests have drowned in this pool. Some who survived reported a strange, dizzying sensation while swimming and the feeling of ghostly hands on their bodies, trying to hold them under the water.'"

Heath shudders. He reaches for the door handle, and something I don't expect happens: the door opens.

I thought for sure we'd locked this room. Having four-year-olds in a place with an unfilled pool that has a twelve-foot drop to hard concrete is a disaster waiting to happen. I'm too surprised to object when he slips inside, pulling me with him.

The room is enormous. Even our footsteps echo in an eerie way. The ceiling is almost entirely made of arched, milky-white skylights, which are now clouded over under piles of snow. In the middle of the room is one of the most enormous lap pools

I'd ever seen. The bottom of the pool is covered with an exquisite stone tile mural of dozens of mermaids. Of course, the pool is empty, the bottom of it cracking so badly that I doubt it would be able to hold much water. Not that I ever had any interest in swimming here, even in the summer. "Ready to go?" I ask Heath, rubbing the chill from my bare arms.

His eyes scan the room. He points to a small door off to the side. "What's in there?"

"Exercise room," I tell him, thinking of the mannequin we'd found there when we first got here. It was lying on a weight bench with a giant barbell across its neck, its head missing, made to look like the ultimate weightlifting accident. I remember laughing when I saw it. It's hard to believe I once found all this stuff as amusing as they made it seem in the brochures. I used to like to run on my mom's treadmill in Boston, but Headless Harry was the reason I never got around to exercising at Bug House, despite the fact that the treadmill worked fine.

"Huh," Heath says, retreating out of the room, much to my relief.

We continue down the hall. At another set of double doors, this time on the right, I stop and pull the doors open, landing us in a ballroom with windows that stretch to the ceiling. There is an enormous fireplace—big enough that a family could stand in it and not have to stoop—on one end. Murals of old pastoral scenes with men and women engaging in all sorts of debauchery cover the opposite wall, while impish little angels cavort in the sky above. Whoever painted these scenes must have been drunk. The pictures on the wall are nearly life-size. I've always thought the people in them looked positively devilish, their eyes wild with madness.

"Wow," Heath murmurs, his voice echoing through the cavernous room. "This is…yet another room that's freaky beyond all reason."

I won't look at the pictures, though the lantern reflects their images in the enormous windows. They freak me out. I cross the dusty parquet floor and head to a small door on the other side of the fireplace.

Heath squints to read the polished plaque. "'After dancing in this ballroom for hundreds of guests, Bella Veronica would retire to this room for a breather. She may have been light on her toes, but sadly, she lost her head after her last performance.'"

He pushes at the door all too eagerly, but I can't share the enthusiasm. There's something on my chest, choking me, making it hard to breathe. Something is wrong here, and I can't quite place what it is. Maybe it's that I've just been kissed. Maybe it's that I've never been in this part of the house after dark. Maybe it's that this house has never seemed so silent and cold.

A rhythmic clicking sound shatters the unearthly silence. I walk behind Heath into a long sunroom that's anything but sunny. It's full of once-white wicker furniture, now yellowed with age, and flowered cushions dulled under layers of dust. The windows are all covered with pink shades. One pane in the window is broken—which is why the room is ice cold—and the curtains are billowing lazily in the corner of the room. But the clicking noise is coming from above.

I've seen this room in the daylight, so I know what the ceiling fans look like. There are six of them spread at similar intervals down the long, narrow room, and the blades are made to look like fronds from an exotic palm tree. They're turning, and the steady clicking and humming mingles with the fierce whistle of wind outside. Maybe at one time the room used to get so much sun that the fans were necessary, but now the room is freezing. I rub my arms and shudder as Heath holds the lantern up.

Then I spy something that I've never seen before, hanging from the fan in the center of the room. I blink again and again, straining to see through the darkness. Is that...

It can't be what I think it is.

Heath must see it at the same time I do, because he sprints forward and stops a few feet away from it.

I step in his shadow until I'm close enough to see that it is, indeed, what I thought it was. Becca's feather boa is tangled in the blades of the fan. It's swaying, looking like a hangman's noose.

I swallow, but my throat is as dry as sandpaper.

"Becca?" he says breathlessly. "Guess Team Yellow got here first."

"Did they?" I ask, looking around the room. I find the switch for the fan buried under the twisted, dry tentacles of a dead hanging plant and flip it off.

"I thought we'd lost power," Heath says, rubbing his chin.

"We have a generator. Some of the wiring is plugged into it as a backup in case power goes out," I tell him, repeating what my mother told me the last time we lost power during a windy night.

"Yeah, but necessary lights and appliances maybe. Fans?"

I know, it's odd, but if I spent time trying to figure out all the mysteries of this place, I'd go insane. As I'm about to tell him that, I notice three envelopes on a glass card table in the corner, under a Siamese cat statue. Red, yellow, and blue. If Becca, Adam, and Liam were here earlier, they forgot their clue. I pick up ours and am easing a thumb under the flap when I see

Heath crouching on the floor underneath the fan. He's pulled the boa down and is staring at it thoughtfully. "What's wrong?" I ask.

I stop short before I get any closer. Directly underneath the fan is a small puddle of blood.

All rooms feature a full bed with a premium mattress, a balcony with delightful scenery (note: balcony not available in the Strawberry Room), plush robes and towels, hair dryers, irons, and ironing boards. Bathrooms are shared (two guest suites to a bathroom). There is a pay telephone located in the lobby.

Gift certificates available. Contact us today!

THIS *is meant to scare us*, I tell myself. This isn't real. This is a game for fun.

But my mom meant to scare us, so congrats to her. It's working. I shiver.

"I think I want this game to be over," I murmur to Heath as he tosses the boa across the room in disgust. I guess blood was matted in the feather boa, because his hands are covered in it.

He wipes them furiously on his pants and nods. He doesn't

look afraid, so maybe he's agreeing because he doesn't want me going mental on him. He stands and puts an arm around me. "God, you're shivering. Come on."

He leads me to the wicker couch and sits me down, then takes off his coat and drapes it over my shoulders. I try to take a breath, but the pressure on my chest crushes me. I can't stop looking at that blood, even though he's coaxing me to look at him. "Hey. Hey. Seda. Look at me. Look right here."

I do. His calmness is contagious. I finally smile, then let out a laugh. "I'm sorry."

"No," he says. "Seriously, this is good. Here I was, thinking you were made of stone."

"My mom said she'd make this scary for us. But this is way beyond what I thought she could do."

He laughs softly. "Well, that's my fault, egging her on to hype it up. We had no idea how far she'd take it. Like Wit said, she's obviously hard-core."

Listening to him laugh is like a dose of the real world, the world outside these creepy walls. I pull his coat tighter around me and stand, trying my best to step over the blood, but it's probably all over the hem of my hoop skirt. I take the next clue and turn it over in my hands, but no matter what I do, I can't bring myself to open it. Even though I know it's all make-believe, I don't want to see what's in the next room. I just want to close my eyes, go to sleep, and wake with the sun.

As if that would end this nightmare on Solitude Mountain.

Heath speaks my thoughts. "Hey. I'm pretty beat. Why don't we go check on your mom? See how she's doing with the food?"

That sounds like the perfect idea. My appetite is pretty much gone, but with the exception of Zoe, my siblings are like Hobbits—they grew up getting a snack every two hours. I get the feeling that all my siblings succumbed to their hunger and are probably in there, begging for tastes of Mom's mashed-potato casserole. The thought of them all gathered around the oven, mouths watering at the sight of the casserole, makes me smile. "Yes. Great. Thanks."

We go back out through the ballroom, and I keep my head down so I won't look at those ghastly figures on the wall. "I'm sorry," I tell Heath once we are clear of them and in the main hallway. "I know you wanted to beat Wit. I guess I'm not much braver than Becca."

"Nah. I don't care. And I'm glad you're scared. To tell you the truth, I'd be more worried about you if you were so used to this place it had no effect on you." He grins. "It's good that you're not desensitized to it. Guess that means you can be saved."

Saved. I look at him. "You think so?"

"'Course. I could tell the second I met you that you didn't belong here."

The pressure on my chest drops to my stomach. Of course he'd think that. He doesn't know about Sawyer. "You…" I stop before I can tell him he doesn't know me. I'd like to live under the delusion that he does. That I don't belong here. At least, for a little while longer.

We reach the foyer. Again, it's as silent as a morgue. And maybe no one, not my siblings, not my mother, belongs in a place like this, where horror movie gore is a fact of everyday life and the line between life and death is constantly blurred. Talk about being desensitized… We don't even bother to look at Silly Sally's bloody heap on the carpet anymore. We just skirt around her like she's a piece of furniture. Heath is the first to arrive at the dining room door. He pushes it, and when it doesn't budge, he knocks. "Dr. Helm?"

Nothing.

"Kids?" I call through the door. "Zain?"

I say his name because I know Zain will be the one giggling on the other side. Adam and Avery will shush him to be quiet, but he won't be able to contain it. He'll be the one bursting out laughing right about now.

Or now.

The silence is more frightening than the most bloodcurdling of screams. I press my ear against the cold walnut door and say a silent prayer that someone, anyone, will answer us.

It doesn't work.

"There's a key," I say softly. I was really, really hoping I wouldn't have to use it. I go to the check-in desk, open the top drawer, shift aside an old reservation book, and pull out a large brass key, like something out of Alice in Wonderland. I hand it to him.

He has to do this, because I can't. I'm too afraid of what lies behind this door.

Heath looks at me, seemingly sensing the fear, though my muscles are working overtime to keep from trembling. He inserts the key in the lock, and it clicks open. He pushes open the door, and we find ourselves in another dark room. The lace tablecloth my mother put out after brunch is still there, but the table isn't set with dinnerware. It's empty.

"Mom?" I call out, already knowing it's futile. I know this even before my eyes trail to the other door, and there is no sliver of light underneath.

I cross the dining room and push open the swinging door to the dark kitchen.

It's not just dark. The room is bare and as unlived in as a museum. The oven isn't warm, and the air smells like lemon dish soap and maple syrup from our brunch. There's not a pot out of place. No one has been down here. No one has been cooking a feast.

But if Mom's not here…

Where else could she be?

I take a few steps toward the center island, then head to the back door. I look out past the ice crystallizing on the window, hoping for some sign of life. Footprints in the snow, something to indicate where my mother has gone. But there's nothing. "She's gone," I whisper.

Heath draws in an uneven breath. "There's a good explanation for this."

If there is one, it doesn't come to me.

"Does your mother usually play around like this?" Heath asks me.

I shrug. As much as she loves all things horror, lately, the extent of her playing is strictly fourth-grade level, like helping us make pillow forts and teaching us those stupid knock-knock jokes. I drop my palms to my side and wipe them on the chiffon of my skirt. "Something is wrong," I whisper, my voice sounding frantic.

"All right, calm down. We'll figure this out." He reverses direction and pushes through both doors to the foyer. He cups his hands around his mouth and calls out, "Wit! Liam! Astrid! Rebecca!"

We listen. I never thought silence could be so frightening. I join in, yelling the kids' names one by one.

Heath draws in a breath and is about to speak when I hear a faint noise.

Giggling.

"Those little bastards," he growls under his breath, then laughs with a relief that I can't share. Because it's too soon to be relieved. Where is my mother? Before I can ask that, he pockets the key and rushes for the steps. He takes them two at a time, while I follow behind him. All the while, the laughter grows louder. When he reaches the top of the steps, he looks around, heading off for the nursery before stopping short.

The laughter is coming from somewhere else. It's…Avery, maybe? Or Zoe. Or…neither. Actually, now that it's closer, it doesn't sound like any of my siblings. It sounds…ghostly. Haunting.

I press myself against the wall as Heath turns around, listening. "Where is it coming from?" He looks at me. "They're playing a trick on us, right? Is everyone in on it but us?"

I gnaw on my lip. My arms hang at my side, powerless to move. I want this game to be over.

He calls for his friends again, and when they don't answer, he throws up his hands. For the first time, he looks like someone other than that easygoing guy who goes with the flow and doesn't let anything rattle him. He doesn't look scared though—not yet. Just annoyed. "This is ridiculous." He comes to my side and plucks the red envelope out of the pocket of the jacket he'd placed on my shoulders. He rips it open and presses his lips together as he reads.

"You know how Orville Redenbacher died? Did he choke on a popcorn kernel?"

Now he sounds angry at me, almost accusing. "I-I don't know."

He drops to his knees and fishes the other two puzzle pieces out of his pockets. He turns them around and manages to fit two together. "Look. Look at this," he says, excitement creeping back into his voice. "I've got something. That letter on the bottom is definitely an *R*. And the picture is...a kid, I think. One of your siblings?"

I kneel down, though it is a bit awkward in my dress, and squint at the puzzle. No. It's not a kid, more like a newborn baby, and all newborn babies look the same, shriveled and red and raisin-like. Really, most of the head is still missing, but the body is there with two tiny clenched fists. But what I recognize is the blanket the baby is swaddled in. It has pink and blue squares. We still have it upstairs, because Zoe uses it for Golly. "No," I tell him. "I think it's me."

"You?" His frown deepens. "So you killed Silly Sally? I have to admit, I'm disappointed. I was hoping this game would be cooler than that. You know, end with a big revelation."

"Like what?" I ask, confused. Frankly, I'm pretty surprised my mom made me the killer. She could've warned me earlier.

He shrugs. "I don't know. Like whoever the killer was, it would make sense. You don't. You have no motive. You're a sweet southern belle. Why would you want to kill Frieda?"

My insides flutter. Even though my family is missing and it's dark and who knows what is going on, Heath's compliment overshadows all of that. That's how out of it I am. Everything's messed up, and he still has the power to make my insides quiver. He doesn't see me stammering to answer him because his gaze wanders across the carpet and stops near the railing. It looks like something one of the kids dropped, but it catches Heath's eye.

He reaches over and picks it up. It's a crumpled piece of paper. He smooths it and shows it to me.

Peter, Peter, pumpkin eater, had a wife and couldn't keep her.

He put her in a _____, and there he kept her very well.

It's written in my mother's slanted handwriting. "I don't understand. This looks like a clue."

"Well, it's not a clue to the game we're playing."

No, it's not, that's for sure. This looks like a clue to the game I thought my mother was going to have us play. Across the hallway, I see the ceramic jack-o'-lantern my mother set out earlier. I walk over to it, reach inside, and find another piece of paper. It says:

Little Miss Muffet...

I look up. "My siblings love these nursery rhymes."

"Maybe there are two games, one for the older kids and one for the younger ones?"

"No. We all had symbols inside our costumes, remember?" I say, a sick feeling creeping over me. "And why was this clue all crumpled up?"

He shakes his head. "I don't know. All I know is that this game is called on account of not making any damn sense." He groans and leans against the railing. "Man, I'm starving."

I reach into the pocket of his jacket and pull out a napkin-wrapped brownie. "Here."

He takes it from me, breaks it in half, and offers me part of it. I shake my head; my appetite's gone. Shrugging, he pops the entire half into his mouth.

Almost at once, he starts to gag.

21

THE INN'S HISTORY

The Bismarck-Chisholm House was built by Nathan Chisholm in 1789. He was a wealthy tobacco magnate who wanted a home in the Allegheny Mountains that would afford him great privacy, since he was a very private man. Upon his death, his nephew, Erik Bismarck, a shrewd businessman, often had people stay in its many unoccupied rooms as they headed west toward California. Knowing this, he added on several wings, until at times, the hotel could house a hundred guests or more. However, the progress of roads and the railroad cut off the house from the main routes of travel, leaving it in virtual seclusion again.

Until the mid-1900s, the house was owned by descendants of the Bismarcks, who ran it as a health resort or sanitarium for the rich and famous who wanted to keep out of the public eye. However, a great fire destroyed one of the wings. The home fell into disrepair. It was bought by the Cooper family, who lovingly restored many of the rooms before their untimely deaths in the 1970s. The current owners, the Fricks, welcome you to this property, as rich in history as it is in mystery. What will you uncover here?

MAYBE if I were at home in Boston, I'd think the brownie had gone down the wrong pipe. After all, Heath coughs once and pounds his chest, his eyes bulging slightly. He doesn't seem too alarmed. But we're in Bug House, and nothing ever goes right here. So my entire body stiffens. I've come to expect the worst.

I start to offer to pat his back when, a moment later, Heath is doubled over, bits of brownie and saliva sputtering from his mouth and dribbling down his chin. He's not really making any sound. I clap him on the back as he heaves and heaves, but it seems so inadequate.

"Do you need water?" I ask stupidly. Can he even answer me? The bathroom is way down the hall anyway. He shakes his head, eyes wide. The Heimlich.

I grab him, from behind and thrust. Once. Twice. Three times. The brownie dislodges, and Heath spits it into his napkin with a gasp. He coughs pieces of brownie and what looks like the sharp edge of a nut into the white fabric. Along with blood, bright-red blood.

Blood. More blood. This time I know it isn't the fake kind.

He falls to his knees listlessly, quiet and exhausted. The clock ticks on below us, echoing around us. The giggling has disappeared.

"Are you OK?" I ask timidly. It seems like a stupid question to ask.

He nods, head still hung low. For the first time, Heath looks defeated. Like he's done with this place.

His voice is scratchy, weak, and high-pitched. "What. The. Hell?" He looks up at me. He reaches for the napkin and runs his finger through the brownie mush. He lifts out a small triangle of glass. He clears his throat, speaking with obvious difficulty. "Oh yeah. Your mother makes the *best* brownies." His words are tinged with sarcasm.

"You don't think she meant to do that!" I say, incredulous.

"What am I supposed to think? She did seem a little off. Way too happy about living here."

He reaches for me, and I flinch as he digs a hand into the pocket of his jacket and pulls out the other brownie. He smashes it in his palm, then pulls out yet another piece of glass. He drops the remnants of the brownie to the ground and holds the tiny hard triangle up to me, right near my face, so I flinch again. "I'll give you that. One piece could be a mistake, Seda. *Not two.*"

"I don't…" What can I say? "My mother would never hurt—"

"Maybe not. But your siblings?"

I shake my head. I let out a shaky breath, thinking of how they love to get a reaction—any reaction—out of people. Avery, especially. She's so competitive and loves to play tricks. But she'd know this was going too far…right?

"Avery!" I shout, heading toward the nursery. "They don't like being alone in the house after dark. Maybe if they got separated, they went in here."

I push open the door and strain to see into their beds. Just then, a strong gust of wind blows against the side of the house, rattling the windowpanes. Heath comes up behind me, shining the lantern into the room. Each of their beds is empty. "Zoe's not here."

I look at him helplessly. "I don't know where else they could've gone."

Heath sweeps the light to a corner of the room.

Curled tight as a ball is Adam. He's shaking. His eyes widen in the light, beneath his halo of platinum hair. He rushes for me, grabbing hold of my middle and toppling me against the door. I hug him tight. His skin is clammy with sweat. "Adam?" I ask him, pushing his blond hair out of his face. "What is it? Where's the rest of your team?"

I've never seen him in such a state. Adam in the calm one, the mature one. Now, all he does is tremble. He doesn't even talk. I pry him from my body and hold him at arm's length. "Adam, do you hear me?"

"Seda," Heath murmurs.

I ignore Heath. Adam does as he's told. The only time he doesn't is when he swears to Avery he'll keep a secret for her. But this is different. There is something so wild and unfocused in Adam's eyes that he almost reminds me of those people in the murals in the ballroom. "Do you know where Avery is?"

"Seda," Heath says again, nudging my shoulder.

I grab Adam tightly by the shoulders and shake him. "Answer me! Why don't you…"

I trail off when I see what Heath must have already seen. The front of Adam's long underwear is drenched in blood.

22

We hope you have a lovely time with us. When (and if) you leave, please fill out a comment card and drop it in the box at the front desk located in the lobby. Luckily, we don't scare many people away for good—we have hundreds of repeat customers!

"IS that real blood?" Heath asks, bringing the lantern close.

"Adam. What is it, sweetie?" I ask him, holding his trembling body to mine. I reach for the nearest blanket and wrap it around him, but he's shaking so hard it won't stay on his shoulders. I look up at Heath. "My mother wouldn't—"

I stop as a voice creeps inside my head. *She wouldn't. But I would.*

Sawyer. I close my eyes. He's been quiet so long that I thought maybe he'd finally gone away. Not for good, because I'm not that lucky. But I thought he'd leave me alone as long as Heath and his friends were here.

Nope, surprise, surprise, I've always been here, Sis. And I told you this would happen. I told you to make them leave, or else.

"Right. Who else could've…?" Heath starts to pace the room. Finally, he stops. "Liam."

I wasn't expecting that name, so when he says it, I feel almost relieved. I look at Adam for some affirmation, but get none. I can't even be sure he's hearing what is being said. He's staring straight ahead, between the Bambi and Thumper pictures on the wall. "Liam? You mean—"

"He's playing some sick game, I'm telling you. Wit likes to joke, but he's harmless. I told you Liam has some screws loose. You know he thought this game was going to be lame, so maybe he wanted to spice it up."

I blink as I look at Adam. "I don't think a joke would have Adam like this."

"He went too far, and your brother here obviously believed it." Heath crouches in front of Adam and taps on his knee. "Hey, buddy. Where's your team? The boy in the mask. Liam?"

Adam swallows and shakes his head, then buries his face in the blanket.

Heath sighs. "Fantastic. What about Becca? The girl with the long, blond hair? You know where she is?"

He doesn't say a thing at first. But when Heath sighs, his small voice drifts out from under the blanket. "Dead."

Heath sucks in a sharp breath, then lets it out slowly. "Come on, kid. Cut it out." When I narrow my eyes at him, he says, "Didn't you say this one is the actor?"

Yes, I did. But Adam has never acted quite so convincingly. Heath still seems to think this is all part of an elaborate joke. That maybe Liam put my little brother up to this. But ever since this night began, there's been something off, as if all the cards have been stacked and now we're just waiting for them to fall. Heath slowly pries the blanket away from my brother's face and says very calmly, "Show me."

My brother shakes his head.

"Please," Heath coaxes, exasperation creeping into his voice.

Adam looks at me. I nod that it's OK. He rocks to his feet and, taking my hand, leads us to the landing, overlooking the foyer. Without looking, he points over the railing, then buries his face in my side. Heath lets out a sigh of relief mixed with annoyance, as in, *Stupid kid, you had us worried for nothing,* since that's where Silly Sally is sprawled. He must think my siblings are so backward that they can't tell pretend from reality.

But we both peer over the railing, past the darkened chandelier, into the grand foyer, with Silly Sally lying in a mangled heap of twisted body parts, her green fringe flapper dress covered in blood. At least, that's what I expected to see, and I'm sure Heath expected the same thing, from the way he wails her name and races for the staircase.

Because the body in the foyer is wearing a red dress. Her hair is splayed out over her pale face, but it is blond, not black.

This isn't Silly Sally.

The body is Becca's.

23

TESTIMONIALS

"I nearly wet my pants, I was so scared, and I didn't
sleep for a week afterward. I loved it!"
—*Bill Evans*

"We had an amazing time for my sister's bridal shower!
Everything was perfect, and the fake blood in the toilet bowls
was a real hoot! We're planning to do it again for my husband's
birthday, because why should we girls have all the fun?"
—*Tiffany Waters*

I DON'T remember descending the staircase. It's all a blur,
my heartbeat thumping in my head, my vision focused on the
body heaped in the center of the round oriental rug. Heath
screams "no" over and over again, but even though he's near me,
he might as well be a thousand miles away. He stops short in
front of Becca, his screaming only growing louder.

"Becca. Oh God." He falls to his knees in front of her.
"Wait! She's alive!" He tries to pull her into his arms.

Blood is everywhere. Becca stares up at him, and for the first time, she doesn't look afraid, just vaguely annoyed because she's trying to speak, but blood is spurting from her mouth like a fountain. Her chest is heaving. She's grasping at her throat, which I can't see through her bloody fingers, but I imagine it's a black hole, as if someone has ripped out her vocal cords.

Decapitated.

"How do we help her? How do we help her?" Heath keeps asking me, but I don't know. All I can think is that I knew this would happen. Nothing ends well on Solitude Mountain.

"Who did this to you?" I ask her, almost afraid to know the answer. Of course, she can't answer. All she is doing now is making gurgling noises, her breathing growing quieter. She closes her eyes, and the ticking of the grandfather clock fills in the ensuing silence. "Is she…dead?"

Heath sets her down gently, then runs his hands through the hair on both sides of his head, not realizing he's getting blood all through his hair. "This isn't happening. This is a joke, right?"

I bend down and pick up the piece of paper on the floor near the skirt of her dress. Before I can open it, I hear Heath behind me, scrabbling with the lock for the front door. He yanks it open and stumbles out onto the front porch. He doubles over, vomiting what's left of the brownies and bile into the snow-covered holly bushes.

"Oh God," he says into the darkness as the snow pelts his face. "Oh God. Who would do this? Liam wouldn't…"

No, of course he wouldn't. And yet Sawyer always knew something bad was going to happen if they stayed. He'd warned me, and I was supposed to warn them. "You should leave."

He sucks in a big gulp of air and stops. His head whips up, and he looks at me like I'm insane. It's funny; it's the way I always expected him to look at me and he never did. He's finally catching on.

"What? What about you?" He starts running his hands through his hair again, but they're sticky and he realizes it, because he's soon wiping them on the front of his pants. He looks back at the house like he'd rather die than go back inside it. I think he's going to throw up again. "I'm not leaving without my friends. This has got to be some horrible mistake, some horrible accident. Like she and Liam were playing around and it went too far."

Just then, Adam appears in the doorway. Heath jumps back and nearly falls over the porch railing. With his hair all crazy, his eyes wild, and his face white, my little brother does look like a ghost. I put an arm around him. His little body feels like a block of ice, even though he's wearing his long underwear. Heath crouches in the snow and peers at him. "You going to tell us what happened yet?"

Adam is still staring straight ahead as if he hasn't heard a word.

"Of course not," Heath sighs. He stares down the driveway for a minute, as if trying to calculate just how long a walk it is to Art's. But the snow is still falling, and some of the drifts are really high. He must decide it's impossible, because he pulls the paper from my hand. It's only in the brightness from the hazy moon on the snow that I realize it's covered with blood. Real blood this time. Though how many times have we trudged through real blood thinking it was fake? Maybe it's been real all the time.

Heath curses under his breath. "Leslie Harvey."

I've never heard the name before. "Do you know who she is?"

"He. A rock musician who was accidentally electrocuted onstage in the 1970s." He faces the house and clenches his fists, steeling himself to go back inside.

That story sounds all too familiar. It's one of the stories about a bedroom upstairs that we'd visited. When he bursts back inside, Heath is so intent on finding the next clue and the killer, or else he doesn't want to see his ex-girlfriend lying there dead, because he doesn't even glance at the spot where Becca is.

Was, actually.

Because that's interesting.

Her body is gone.

24

The housekeeping staff, the waitstaff, the concierge…
every member of our staff is frightfully good at what
he or she does. We employ some of the finest perform-
ers you'll ever see. Or are they performing? One thing
is for sure: they are all classically trained in the art of
scaring the pants off our guests.

I DOUBLE-TIME it and somehow manage to reach
Heath while he's only halfway up the stairs. I tug on his sleeve
to get him to slow down. When he does, he whirls back, half
annoyed, half frantic. He follows my line of vision and nearly
slips off the step. Grabbing hold of the handrail, he leans forward to get a better look, almost like he can't believe what he's
seeing. I can't.

Heath doesn't say anything for a full ten seconds, as if his
mind is still trying to process it all. He teeters back and forth
on his feet, grasping the railing, as if he's about to topple over.

Finally, he asks, "What the hell is going on?"

I don't answer until he turns and looks at me, as if he's expecting me to. "I don't know," I say dumbly.

"Did someone simply pick up her body and move it? Did she get up and walk away?" He looks at me and then at Adam. "Did you guys see anyone? How did we not notice?"

Adam's face is expressionless. He's not helping at all. "It was too dark," I fill in.

"Well, that's just perfect," Heath mumbles, continuing up the steps.

When we get to the top of the stairs, I notice Adam shuffling on his feet. I've seen that particular dance before. He's holding the front of his pants. I take his hand. "I have to take him to the bathroom."

Heath gives me that incredulous look again. "Becca was just…" He stops. "What the hell is going on with you, Seda? Do you understand what's going on here?"

I look at him. "What do you—?"

"I don't know what's happening, but I don't think we need a potty break right now."

"Well, Adam does," I snap at him, surprised by the strength in my voice. "If you want to keep playing this game, you go ahead. I have to take him to the bathroom."

"Game? Screw the game!" That look again. It's starting to become permanent.

"What do you want me to do?"

"I want you to… Jeez, Seda. Give a shit, maybe? My friend just died. And then her body disappeared. Some seriously messed-up shit is going on, and you act like you've been taking a walk in the park."

He's right. Maybe because I expected this, warned them against this. Sawyer warned something terrible would happen if they stayed. I look at Adam, who's fidgeting even more. "I'm sorry. But he really needs to go."

Heath studies me, then shifts the lantern to his other hand and grabs hold of one of the gargoyle candlesticks. Hefting its substantial weight, he switches direction. "Fine. But we go together. No more splitting up."

I stare at the candlestick in his hand. It reminds me of when I found him standing in the kitchen, holding the bloody prop ax, getting ready to pop whatever animal was in the kitchen over the head with it. "What are you going to—" I stop before I can ask the stupid question. "What if you run into one of my siblings? You could hurt them."

He lets out a shaky breath, and that incredulous look creeps once again into his expression. He doesn't drop his weapon, which tells me he's starting to become afraid of me.

Now he's starting to understand.

"Follow me," he says.

I follow him, holding tight to Adam's hand. Before we get to the door of the bathroom, I expect to hear the hollow sound of the bathtub and sink faucets dripping in odd intervals—*drip-drip, drip-drip*—against rusty porcelain. Instead, the dripping is different, like the water is splashing into an already full bowl. I stop. Adam senses something is amiss too, because he wrenches my wrist away and plants his feet next to mine.

Heath carries on another couple of steps before he realizes I'm not with him.

When he turns, I shake my head slowly, my expression warning.

Holding the lantern out in front of him, he positions himself squarely in front of the half-closed bathroom door. Then he kicks it open. It crashes against the doorstop and nearly slips closed again, but Heath stops it with the candlestick and pushes inside.

He retreats almost instantly, dropping the lantern on the ground and wailing. He kicks the wall and bites his closed fist. He sinks to a crouch, hunched over, still letting out a horrible guttural sound deep within his throat. "Wit's dead."

I gasp. My eyes trail to the door. It's open, and in daylight I could possibly see inside, but now that it's dark, I can only see the discolored tile around the door, disappearing into shadow, and what could be a bloody handprint. Do I want to see more? "Are you—"

"Yeah." Heath clears his throat. "He's in the bathtub. You don't want to go in there. There's so much blood."

25

Turn-down service is available after 6:00 p.m., but we advise those who *don't* partake of this service to *always* check under your covers, under your bed, and in any closets. You never know what lurks in the darkness…

I STAND in the doorway, bracing myself to look inside. But what good would seeing the carnage do? In the end, I drop my fists to my side and look up at Heath. His expression doesn't give me any comfort. He's pale, holding the lantern again and spinning in circles as if he expects the assailant to come out of nowhere and kill us.

In the silence that follows, I hear the soft rushing of water. There's a small stream at my feet. The front of Adam's pants are wet. The worst part of it, though, is that he doesn't even seem to realize he's peed himself. He's staring ahead, unmoving, unblinking.

"Liam was in the bathroom earlier," Heath whispers. "Remember?"

You were too, Sawyer adds. I swallow. I wonder what it will take for Heath to remember that and turn against me. "When I was in there before, all I saw were the clues on the windowsill. Nothing else."

He doesn't say anything.

"I have to find my brother and sisters," I say with urgency.

"No. You're coming with me." Heath's voice is hard-edged. "Wait! Stop!"

I whirl around. He's staring at something down the hall. But there's nothing there now. "What did you see?"

"I thought I saw someone." Heath grabs my hand and pulls me and Adam down the hallway, stopping short in the middle of it. "It was here. Someone was crouching here. I'm sure of it. And now he's gone."

"Gone?" My ears prick up. I run my hand down the wall, feeling for the lever. In the dark, it's not so easy, but there's a small indentation in the wainscoting. I press it, and to his astonishment, a small, square hole opens up in the wall, barely large enough for an adult to fit through on their hands and knees.

We both stoop to peer inside. We were in darkness before. Inside the wall is even bleaker. It's an absolute abyss. We listen for a moment, and maybe my ears are playing tricks on me, but it sounds like dying footsteps echoing deep within the passage. "Did you hear that?" Heath asks me.

I nod.

"What is in here?"

"It's a passage to another wing," I whisper. "The kids use it, mostly. It's too tight for most people."

He swallows and holds the lantern in front of him, past the opening. I suck in a breath as he crawls in on his hands and knees, filling the entire opening with his thick body. I'm cringing at the thought of going inside, when he retreats, holding something in his hands. It's a scrap of gray fabric.

No, that's not what it is. It's the gothic maid's uniform my mother had on, and it too is splattered in blood.

My breath catches as he calls into the void: "Doctor Helm!"

But I know she won't answer. Whoever is in there is running away and doesn't want to be seen. I look over at Adam, who is shivering. "Mommy's OK," I tell him, forcing a smile. "Don't worry."

He isn't even looking at the uniform though. He's staring at his feet.

Heath sighs. "I don't think I can fit in there. Where does it let out?"

"I'll show you." Heath shoves the bloody uniform back

inside, and we make our way to another wing. When we get to the other end of the tunnel, the hallway is deserted.

"Dead end. Literally," Heath mutters, punching the wall. He slumps against it, and for a minute, he's completely silent. Then he says, "I think I know where they are."

"You do?" I ask doubtfully.

Heath reaches into his pocket and pulls out the crumpled sheet of paper. "Astrid was the rock star," he says in a dull monotone. "Don't you see? He's killing people based on the way they're dressed. Becca was dressed like that dancer. And Wit was dressed like Orville Redenbacher. Astrid said something about his crappy snack food. I don't know for sure how he died, but I bet it was in a bathtub."

"So that means..." I don't know what it means. That anyone could be so evil is unconscionable, because it means that they've taken a game and are killing for the pure joy of it. For sport. I knew there was evil in this house, but I didn't know it could make someone so inhuman, so sadistic. So...*like Sawyer.*

"It means..."

Why can't I get my mouth to form actual words around him, anymore? Why can't I react like Becca would, screaming her head off? Heath had nudged me out into the light, but I knew it wouldn't last. Now, I'm standing here, teeth chattering, retreating farther and farther into my shell, to the point where Boston and friends and normal life will be impossible.

His friends are dead, and this is my house and my fault. I should've tried harder to warn them.

We step cautiously down the hall. When we reach the room, Heath grimaces at the closed door. "Leslie Harvey was a rock star, and he was electrocuted," he says, pointing to my shoulder.

Every pore on my body is a goose bump, and some of my hair is standing straight on end, crackling with static. He studies the doorknob, as if contemplating whether to touch it. Finally, he backs up and kicks in the door.

The second he does, I smell something I've never smelled before. It's a sickly sweet, smoky scent…burning flesh? I wouldn't know what that smells like. He doesn't go inside. He stands in the doorway, his body slumped in an unnatural way for someone I thought was so strong, so invincible. He turns to me, the candlestick in his hand, and starts to say something, but stops when he spies something over my shoulder.

I whirl around just in time to see a figure in a mask and cape, swooping down the hallway away from us.

"Liam!" Heath screams at his friend, but the caped figure only speeds up.

But is it really his friend? It's Liam's costume, Liam's cape, but he disappears down the steps in utter blackness with hardly a sound, which is more than I could do. I'd probably bump into things or trip over my own feet, it's so very dark.

But he does it with the grace and ease of someone who's lived within these walls much of his life.

Not a visitor.

Not Liam.

26

HOUSE RULES

- Guests are welcome to explore any area of the house except the individual guest rooms. Also, some areas are marked off with yellow tape. For your safety, please keep out of those marked areas.
- Please be courteous to other guests. We all have to live (and die) together, so let's make the best of it.
- Any issues, please report them to the front desk immediately.

"COME on," Heath urges me, impatient. He shouts, "Liam!" loud enough to rattle the chandelier crystals in the foyer.

Heath races down the hallway and barrels down the staircase. I reach the top landing in time to see the figure race across the foyer toward the kitchen. When I reach the bottom of the stairs, instead of following Heath, I lunge for the doors to the Safe Room, hoping I can tuck Adam in there. I shouldn't be surprised that they're locked. Of course. No one is really safe here.

I yank Adam along with me and push open the door to the dining room. Heath is standing in the kitchen, breathing hard and looking at the closed back door. "I thought he went this way," he says.

I peer out the window. Not only is the snow smooth and untouched by humans, but the drifts in the back of the house are nearly halfway up the door. "I did too."

His eyes scan the kitchen, first landing on the knife block. He pulls out the biggest butcher knife of the set. It gleams in the light as he holds it up. When I look up again, his eyes are fastened on the freezer. He juts his chin toward it. "You think he's in there?"

I shake my head. "No, he's—"

"Come on, Seda. You have been hiding something from us in there all this time. What is it?"

"Nothing, I—" I stop. "Like I said, we don't want the kids getting any ideas. Besides, I don't know where the key is."

He doesn't believe me. I can tell from the disappointment on his face, the way he gets this crinkle on his forehead. He sets the lantern down on the counter and throws up his hands in exasperation. "You were in there yesterday," he says. "When I first met you."

"I-I was?" It all comes back to me. *I was.*

Now he looks at me like I'm insane. He's suspicious. His eyes narrow. I knew it was only a matter of time before he turned against me. He opens his mouth to say something, but as he does, a shadow moves in the window outside. He tilts his head, glides closer to the window, and pushes aside the curtain.

"You said that wing over there isn't being used?"

"Yes. It was burned out in the 1970s after a fire—"

"Well, someone's using it," he says. He lifts the curtain further so I can peer through the frosted glass.

Sometimes, on warm summer nights, I'd look out this window and see absolutely nothing but blackness, not even stars, because the trees would always get in the way. The moonlight would even fade, shielded by the overhang of the roof and arms of the house. But now, amid darkness upon more snowy darkness, in the far-off distance of that unused wing, where the mountain might as well drop off into absolute nothingness… glows a faint, steady light.

"Lying hasn't worked for you, Seda," Heath mumbles. "Maybe you should try telling me the truth."

I open my mouth to protest, but he's right. If I'd been truthful with him, maybe I'd have already told him about the freezer. After all, he's the closest person I have to a friend up here. "I still talk to Sawyer sometimes," I say softly.

He stares at me. "Sawyer. You mean, the twin brother you never had?"

I nod. "Like I said, I absorbed him in the womb, so sometimes I feel like he's inside me. And I got this feeling that he didn't want you here. I know it sounds crazy. But that's why I wanted you to leave. He's my sense when bad things are going to happen."

Heath stares at me for the longest time, and I wait for the disgust to creep in. It doesn't. He doesn't speak. He doesn't yell at me or tell me I'm not batshit crazy. Instead, he takes a step back and twists the lock for the back door.

"Wait. Where are you going?" I ask in a panic.

"Where do you think?" He doesn't even look at me, his voice is edged with sarcasm. "Aren't you even the least bit interested in who killed my friends?"

I fight back the urge to tell him to go to hell. "You can't go that way." Which is the truth; the snow is so high he'd need to tunnel his way out of the drift. "Come this way."

He pauses for a moment, looking like he isn't sure whether to trust me, then follows me out into the foyer. We both look at the spot where Becca was, almost as if we're wondering who will be there next. But the carpet is empty. I pull aside the plastic covering and point the way.

The burned-out wing is not completely concealed from the elements, since the walls are partially collapsed and the roof is caved in in places. But the structure that remains is a good barrier against the wind and has kept out a lot of the snow. When Heath steps over the threshold into the cold, the snow barely covers his boots.

It feels strange, going this way, after so many of my mother's warnings to stay out. Adam's hand tenses in mine; he must be thinking the same thing. She told us there were too many rusty nails and broken pieces of glass to hurt ourselves on, and though it's true, it really isn't that much more dangerous than the rest of the house. I sandwich Adam between Heath and me, where it's safest, holding his hand and helping him over the charred rafters and debris. Even without the heavy gusts of wind, it's bitter cold, and I'm breathless, choking on icy air and bits of floating ash. All the while, I strain past the lantern light to see a sign of the other light, the one we'd spied in the distance. But there is nothing.

Suddenly Heath stops. "Look here. This is how I got into the house yesterday," he mumbles. "But I know I didn't make all these prints."

He shines the lantern low, illuminating a patch of snow between the debris. There are large footprints there, a mess of them. This is a well-traveled path—for someone, at least. An owl shrieks from the rafters above, flapping his wings loudly, and Adam pulls me closer as we navigate away from the main body of the house.

Eventually, the blackened part of it gives way to a section of the house that seems virtually untouched by the fire, if not by the elements. Old, dead vegetation is creeping up the sides of the walls, and the wooden floors have been damaged—likely by rain—but they're not covered in soot, and the windows still have glass in their panes. There's a single white wall standing in front of us, with an old, framed pastoral painting hanging there, rippled with age.

"I have never been into this part of the mansion," I say, breathing out.

I don't know if Heath doesn't believe me or doesn't care—or both. He points wordlessly to a small alcove in the corner. There, I can make out a railing, and the beginning of a narrow staircase.

We creep to the bottom of it, and he holds the lantern out, shining it as far into the stairwell as possible. It rises to a small closed door. Underneath shines a small sliver of light. Heath opens his mouth to say something, just as we hear a faint creaking noise from within, like footfalls on the floorboards.

Someone is up there.

27

Would you like to know how a typical murder mystery evening unfolds? The following is based around a three-course meal, but we're more than happy to fit in with whatever suits your tastes best. All timings are flexible, and all sorts of variations on this basic structure are possible!

7:30 p.m.   Guests assembled; actors arrive in character and start mingling

7:40 p.m.   Brief MC speech sets the scene; all guests have programs with background info and clues throughout the event— scenes take place between the actors, and the audience are invited to eavesdrop; actors are always in character and can be quizzed by guests at any time

8:00 p.m.   Starter served; more scenes follow

8:30 p.m.   Main course served; more scenes follow

9:00 p.m.   Dessert served; a murder occurs

9:30 p.m.   Audience interrogate suspects

9:45 p.m.   Audience try to work out "whodunit"

10:00 p.m. Perpetrator revealed; champagne and prizes for winner(s)

10:15 p.m. Event concludes

I DON'T understand. I'd seen this part of the wing still standing, but I assumed it was abandoned, like the rest of the wing. When we lived in Boston, any time an apartment was vacated, squatters would inevitably try to find their way in. It seems impossible that squatters would find their way up the mountain to take shelter here.

The stairwell is so narrow that Heath's broad shoulders graze the walls on each side. He treads gently, but with every step comes a creak that sounds much too loud. When he reaches the top, he peers down at me for a second, then presses the latch atop the door handle and pushes open the slatted wooden door. He steps into the room and lowers his lantern, then disappears inside.

Holding Adam close, I climb the next step so that I can peer in. The room is definitely lived in. There's an oil lamp on a table, a small bed, and other items. In fact, this room looks cozier than mine, that's for sure. My eyes catch on a garbage can, filled with discarded wrappers for my mother's favorite organic granola bars. Oddly, the whole room has a familiar scent, a familiar feel to it, almost like déjà vu.

One thing is clear. Whoever has been staying here isn't here now. The window is open a crack, and news clippings are scattering across the floor. A rocking chair with bunnies on it, like one you'd find in a nursery, is slowly rocking back and forth in the breeze and must have been the source of the creaking we'd heard outside. I steady it as Heath motions me forward. "You said you had a twin brother."

"No. He wasn't real. I only sometimes—" I stop when I look down at the book in his hands. It's an old battered photo album, with an embossed leather cover.

In one of the photos is a picture of me as a baby. It's the same picture that I thought was on the back of the clues we'd been getting. But…it's not me. The blanket the baby is wrapped in says *Sawyer*.

Heath flips a page, and a piece of paper slides out. I pick it up and unfold it. I know that handwriting. It's my mother's.

Dear Aunt Ellie,

I am so sorry that it has been such a struggle of late. As I told you in my last letter, we are doing everything possible to change the situation. I understand that things are difficult, which is why Sawyer is there with you and not with us. I have been looking into nursing homes, but they seem so inhumane.

Despite what he did to Seda, he's just a child. We feel very strongly he needs to be with family, or else he'll spend the rest of his life in an institution.

I wish we had some way of communicating other than these letters. I feel so far away from you and from him, so helpless. But for Seda's sake, you know we could not continue to keep him under our roof.

Thank you for the pictures. He is growing so fast that it hurts my heart not to be able to be there with him. Let him out of the restraints on his good days, would you? Enclosed is some money for his care.

I love you and appreciate everything, as always,
Maya

I read the words over and over again. I'm about to read them one more time when a voice says, "What if he wasn't in your imagination, Seda? What if he's real?"

I'm jarred out of my thoughts, which are running along

that same track. "That's ridiculous," I say, the paper shaking in my hands. I look down at the photo. It looks like me. I thought it was me, without the name on the bottom. "There's got to be some other explanation."

"Like what?" Heath asks, flipping the page. "He wasn't inside you, Seda. He's real. Your mother kept your twin brother a secret from you all this time."

With that, I double over as a sharp pain grips my stomach. All this time…the twin I thought was inside me was living three states away? Not only that, but he had violent tendencies that demanded she keep him apart from me? But did she have to keep him a secret from me too? Is that even possible? "I'd remember him."

"Maybe. Maybe not. I don't remember most of my life before I was three. Maybe everyone convinced you that he was your imaginary friend."

I think of the suggestions Sawyer gave me when I was a child. Did they come from inside me, or had they come from someone living? *You have a real good imagination.* Those words in my mother's voice. She was always trying to protect us, but more than anything, she wanted to keep us together. I'm suddenly struck with something I heard her whisper to my father one night before he left: *Above all, we have to stay together.* I take a deep breath of air, and another, but it doesn't help. The room is spinning, and my vision bends. "Heath, this is ridiculous. She couldn't…"

I trail off. *Maybe she could.*

I steady myself against the edge of the table as Heath says, "Hey, look at this."

I don't want to see more, but he shoves it under my nose so that I have no choice but to read. It's a small news clipping with the headline "Couple Found Murdered in Remote Mansion." I scan the article, catching on the sentence, "State Police have no leads as to who could have committed these brutal murders…" My eyes sweep over the smiling faces of a gray-haired couple in the black-and-white photo beside the article.

I've never seen pictures of them before, but I can only guess that these people are my aunt and uncle. My mother never said how they died. I'd assumed it was from old age, but what if they had been murdered? Would she have come here to watch over Sawyer and never told us? It all sounds so utterly unbelievable, but at the same time, I've read stories about how twins communicate. Maybe the feeling in my stomach wasn't Sawyer speaking from inside me, but from somewhere else.

I shove the article back into the book before I can read more. I swallow back the lump in my throat and lurch away. I'm going to throw up.

"My twin brother is really alive," I murmur. "Alive, and a serial killer."

My own flesh and blood was born insane. But at least he's not me. We may have shared a womb, but twins are different people. He's not a part of me. And maybe, if that's true, then…

Heath doesn't say a word. He's still flipping through the photo album. I don't want to look, but it's like I can't turn away. There are more baby pictures, and then the same photo I had in my bedroom upstairs, with the seven of us together last Christmas at our home in Boston. I don't have to look closely to see that there is a big, fat X drawn in Sharpie over every one of our faces.

The one over mine looks particularly heavy.

Sawyer hates us, but he hates me most. I have no doubt about that. He's probably killed my mother by now, and all my siblings. Maybe he's saving me for last.

I grab Adam's hand tightly as the realization overcomes me. *Sawyer is responsible for all the deaths in this house. I had nothing to do with any of this.*

But he's not done yet. I've always known that Sawyer hated me. And yet, despite that, my stomach feels settled with relief. *It's not me.*

"If your brother's doing this, where the hell is Liam?"

"Dead," I say surely. "I'm sure it has to do with whatever costume he had on and that gunshot we heard."

"Gunshot?" Heath says as if he'd forgotten.

But for me, it's like a window shade that was stuck halfway is now opened fully, letting in all the light. Everything makes sense. Why my mother was oddly protective of us. Why we spent time in Erie when we first got down here. Why she'd disappear for hours and we'd think she was in her office writing. All those weekly trips she'd take down to Art's. Why we had to stay. Why Dad was so upset before he…

Heath slumps down on the bed and buries his head in his hands. "Oh yeah. That's right. *Shit. Shit, shit, shit.* We've got to get out of here. The three of us can make it down the mountain. That's got to be safer than being here."

I shake my head furiously. "I can't go without my family."

"What if they're dead?"

"What if they're not?" I reply. "I can't just leave them."

"Right. Shit." He rubs at his eyes tiredly. "You know he's going to kill us, one by one. Right?"

I grip the knife's handle. "Not if we stay together."

He brings his hands together in front of his mouth, almost as if praying. Finally, he nods and stands, rubbing his hands together. "All right. Let's go get them."

"OK." I start for the door and suddenly stop.

Adam is gone.

28

WHAT WE GUARANTEE

We run our hotel with one simple goal: to be the best
and most unique murder mystery hotel in the business.
For the past fifteen years, we've succeeded, attracting
guests from all across the country! *Philadelphia* magazine named us a Top Unique Destination of 1993!
We guarantee strong murder mystery story lines, great
set pieces, and vivid characters with a full cast of out-
standing actors. We also provide advance information,
allowing guests to choose their level of involvement
and to play along as much as they wish. Any special
requests you have can be easily incorporated into the
script! We'll even create a brand-new event, based on
your suggestions. Ask about the option of a profes-
sionally edited video containing highlights of your
weekend, for an additional fee!

"ADAM!" I whisper-shout against the wind as we make our
way back to the main part of the house. In the light of the
lantern, I see what I think are his footprints in the snow. Even

though he has big feet, they're smaller than the average adult male's. Why did he leave? Particularly after he knew that we weren't alone? That Sawyer was inside? I thought he was smarter than that.

Two things happen in the next couple of seconds. The lantern goes out, and Heath lets out a low moan of agony. I bump into his frame. He's doubled over. "What?"

"Shit. Shit," he says, falling over onto his side. There's not even moonlight to help us see. "I got my leg caught on a piece of glass. I'm bleeding."

I crouch and splay my hands through the dark, feeling for him. I come in contact with the fabric of his shirt, his warm body. "Can you move?"

"Yeah. I'll be OK." I hear him struggling to stand. I manage to get an arm underneath his body and help him to his feet. "Damn. Can't see anything now. We need light."

I try to think of where we have a flashlight, but the only thing I can think of is the oil lamp my mom was using to paint trim, which I remember her doing last in the Strawberry Room. "There's a lamp and matches in one of the bedrooms upstairs. I can go—"

"We go together." His voice is firm. "Stay close to me."

It's slow work, making our way through absolute dark. He

trudges through at a snail's pace, his breathing labored, suggesting he's in more pain than he's letting on. He helps me over whatever obstacles are in the way, until finally I can hear the plastic door covering crackling in the breeze. When we reach it and climb inside, I say, "Let me lead. I know this place better than you."

"Hold on a second." He falls to the ground, none too gracefully. "I need to wrap this. I'm bleeding everywhere, and my knee's swollen up like a balloon."

"OK." I point to the kitchen. "I'll just…"

"Together." His words come out through teeth that are obviously gritted in pain. He's already trying to get to his feet. I lead him into the kitchen, where I lean him against the center island as I open cabinets and retrieve a dishrag. He'll need an ice bag too. I cross past the ovens and fumble with the canisters, trying to find the right one. When I get the key out of the smallest canister, I make my way toward the freezer door.

"Are you going to be OK?" I ask him when he lets out a yelp.

"Yeah. Fine," I hear him mutter.

"I always worried about something terrible like this happening," I say as I twist the key. I pull open the door and hear the pop of suction. The freezer walls aren't whirring and vibrating because the generator doesn't power the freezer, but it's just as cold inside. Tucking the key into the pocket of Heath's jacket I'm wearing, I take a deep breath. I have to tell him. He saw Sawyer's room. He'll believe me. And if I don't do it now, I'll never have the courage.

"Ever since August...I think something happened with Sawyer when my dad was here. I think Sawyer killed my father."

There was a long pause. The darkness distorted time, which seemed to stretch for forever. "What?" Heath asks.

I reach around, fumbling near the meats for the ice trays. "I'd had an argument with my dad, because he wanted to leave and go back to Boston. I knew my mother wanted us to stay together. That's what she always said. He wanted me to talk some sense into her. I woke up one night after they'd had a really brutal fight, came downstairs to make some warm milk because I couldn't sleep. I..." I swallow, and my lips tremble at the memory.

"I found him in the kitchen. I had this feeling inside that I was somehow connected to him lying there, but I couldn't remember anything. Sawyer kept saying my name though, over and over again. I was terrified of what I had done, what Sawyer had done from inside me. So I cleaned it up. I drove his car out into the lake and threw all his suitcases in there too. When I was done, I knew I needed to kill myself. To kill Sawyer.

"I drew a bath, and while I was washing off all the blood, I tried to drown myself. But I couldn't. I didn't know if it was because I was too much of a coward or because he wouldn't let me."

Heath doesn't say anything for a while. Then his voice cuts through the darkness. It's calm. "You…put your father's body in the freezer, didn't you?"

I shudder. As terrible as it is, it's almost freeing to tell someone else. "Yes. In the back. My mother and siblings don't even know. She thinks my father left in the middle of the night, and that he's still in Boston, ignoring her because of their fight. But now that I know Sawyer did it, it all makes sense."

Again, silence. I hear something slide against a countertop and footfalls on the floor. He can't keep doing this to me. Every time he doesn't answer, I think maybe Sawyer has gotten to him. "Heath?"

"You're kidding, right? This is all a joke, right, Seda? Your mother put you up to it?"

"What?" How could he think I'd joke about a thing like this, after all that's happened? I turn to look at him, but of course I can't see his face. His voice seems closer. "He's over by the…"

I can't remember. The body's way in the back, where I never go. I've never ventured that far into the freezer again. I could offer to show Heath, but it's not like we could see anything. Just then my hand grazes the familiar. I pull out one of my siblings' boo-boo buddies, victorious. Someone makes a guttural sound, and I freeze.

Complete silence.

I whirl. "Heath?" I call from the threshold of the freezer.

All I hear are the muffled ticks of the clock, outside in the foyer. *Oh no.*

Then I venture the name that seems so much more possible now. "Sawyer?"

Suddenly, someone plants their hands on my shoulders, shoving me hard. I stumble backward, my shoulder hitting the shelving unit before I crash to my backside. I hear the sound of the door creaking shut.

I'm being shut in.

"Wait!" I lunge toward the door and manage to get my arm through when the door closes hard on it. Pain screams up my arm, and I let out a scream. Someone is bearing down on the door with all his weight. "Stop! My arm!"

Did I think Sawyer would ever stop? He doesn't care about breaking my arm. He wants me dead. I wedge my foot through the opening and push with the whole of my body. I feel it budge a little, and I wedge more of my body in. Now I'm half in and half out of the freezer. I'm summoning strength I never knew I had, because the alternative is too horrible to contemplate.

I give the door a final shove and burst out, running headlong into the side of the center island. My hands scrabble on the countertop, trying to come up with a weapon. The first thing I find is the tea canister. Grabbing it, I whirl backward and slam it into Sawyer's head. It stuns him enough to allow me to shove him back through the doorway.

"*Seda!*"

Wildly, I grab the door handle and shove the freezer closed, leaning on it with all my weight as I secure the lock.

My eyes sweep uselessly around the dark kitchen as pounding thuds on the door behind me. The door is so thick that it muffles the noise. From here, it sounds harmless and faraway, like raindrops on a roof. I'm safe. Sawyer can't get out. At least, I hope. But that's what I used to think before, when I thought he was inside me. And now he's here.

"Heath?" I call, daring to hope he may still be alive.

No answer.

First Adam, and now Heath. I'm alone.

So much for staying together.

29

Want to get in touch with us? Please don't hesitate to call or fax us at the numbers on the back of this brochure. We promise you the event of a lifetime!

LET *me know if you can talk some sense into her.*

Those were the last words my dad ever said to me.

They'd been screaming at each other all day. My father kept saying school was starting, Seda needs to be there, and my mother said that she wouldn't leave until a suitable buyer was found and the house was sold, that she'd already written the school for my homework, that she had her book to finish and her sabbatical wasn't officially over until January first. At one point, my mother pushed my father so violently that he almost fell down the stairs. After that, he looked at her, hate in his eyes, and started to pack his suitcase.

Hours later, I'd gone down to the kitchen to get some milk. Everyone was asleep. He came in and started piling his beer from the refrigerator into a crate, telling me he was sorry, but he couldn't live like this. It was such a cliché that I would've laughed, if I hadn't seen the emotion in his eyes.

I knew he wasn't coming back. I couldn't stand it. I begged him. I told him, through sobs, that our family needed to stay together. I told him he would destroy us if he left us.

He finished piling the beer into the crate and looked at me ruefully. *Let me know if you can talk some sense into her.*

I remember walking to the back door as he carried the crate to the car, pulling my robe over my shoulders and looking out at the blackest of nights, thinking how typical of them, leaving the fate of their marriage in *my* hands. I remember the creak of the hinges on the old screen door, the sound of the bullfrogs thrumming in the lake beyond, and...Dad coming back to do a last sweep of the house to make sure he wasn't forgetting anything.

The next thing I knew, he was on the kitchen floor, sprawled out on his back like a sunbather. There was blood. Too much blood. It seeped around my bare toes. The ax handle stood up from the center of his chest, the white golf shirt I'd bought him for Christmas completely ruined. Even in death, his expression never lost that look of abject surprise, suggesting he hadn't expected death in the least.

My mind spiraled. I'd opened my mouth, called out for Mom. Of course, the house was so big she didn't hear. Then my mind whirled out further. I couldn't recall pulling the ax out from the woodpile behind the house or swinging it. Maybe it was my imagination, but the more I stared at my father's body, the more I could feel splinters from the wooden handle, digging into my palms. No one else could've done it. It *had to* have been me.

I would be arrested. My mom would be blamed for not seeing the signs. For not making me keep up my visits with Dr. Batton. Isn't that what always happened? The loved ones get blamed, always suffer most.

Our family would be torn apart. My mother would be destroyed.

When that thought hit me, I knew I couldn't let it happen.

Slowly, another idea took root in my head. I stood up, fished around in the tea canister, and pulled out the key to the freezer. I unlocked the freezer and pulled him in. I scrubbed away every trace of blood. Then I went outside, drove his car to the edge of the pond, put it in neutral, and shoved. Back at the house, I found his suitcase in the front hall, so I dragged it down the hill and threw it in there too. When it was all done, when every trace of my father had been removed from sight, I took a bath. I washed it all away, then I sank underneath the water and tried to drown myself.

I couldn't do it. As much as I wanted to die, to kill the monster inside me, I couldn't.

And maybe this is why. Maybe some invisible hand lifted me out of the water, protected me, *so that I could kill him now.*

"Heath?" I call again, stepping forward blindly, feeling my way as I walk. I expect to bump into his motionless body with every step. Before long, I reach the door to the kitchen. I push it open. The house is so silent. Even the grandfather clock seems to have stopped ticking. I'm alone. Really, truly alone.

What the hell am I going to do? I can't stay here with all these dead bodies until spring.

Taking a few deep breaths, I force myself to concentrate. Light. I need to find light. I climb the stairs and stumble down the hallway into the Strawberry Room. As I do, I think of the plaque outside the door. It's one so horrific that I have it committed to memory: *The Strawberry Room belonged to Esther Wise in 1928. She was a famous actress who burned to death when someone intentionally set her elaborate costume on fire, and she couldn't escape from it in time.*

A fierce wind rocks the house as I reach the door. I step inside and manage to find the lantern atop the rickety old night table. My hands pat down the table's worn surface, searching out the box of matches I'd last seen there.

But they're gone.

I hear a scratching sound behind me, and the whoosh of fire being lit. "Looking for these?"

I turn. Standing in the doorway, holding a single lit match and the matchbox, is a man in a cape and the horrid mask with the twisted nose and sunken, skull-like eyes. I know who this is, and it's the reason why I can't feel relief, even after I'd shut and locked the freezer door. In horror movies, that relief is always short-lived. I knew Sawyer would manage a way out. He's like Jason or Freddy or Michael Myers: immortal, unstoppable.

"Sawyer?" I ask timidly.

"Nice to meet you, Sister. Though we have met before, even if you don't remember it." His voice is calm and pleasant, as if this really is a happy family reunion. I can't see his face, but I know he is smirking. I know so much about him that it's scary. And I know that he meant for me to be here now. He meant to kill me last.

"The game didn't go exactly as I planned," he says calmly. "And certainly not as well as Mother had planned. But that's all right. She left me to rot here all those years, while she went off with you. So I'd say this is only fair. Our game is working out just fine, wouldn't you say?"

How do I answer that? My vocal cords are frozen. He steps closer to me and lights the lantern. I'm sure he can hear my heart beating a million miles an hour. If I know so much about him, then he definitely knows how terrified I am of him. There's no use in fighting it. I know he's going to kill me, so there's no use in begging for my life. The best thing to do is stay silent.

"Don't cry, Seda," he says almost kindly as I realize there are tears on my cheeks. "Or should I say *Martha*?"

He laughs like he's just told the funniest joke ever.

"Oh, you don't get it, do you? That's who you are. Martha Mansfield. When you all chose your costumes, you chose how you're going to die. And Martha, you see...she was a famous actress who died like the woman on the plaque in this room. She was on set for a Civil War film, wearing a costume much like yours, when her dress suddenly burst into flames. They say someone threw a match at her."

I gasp, staring helplessly at the match in his hand, burning down to his pale fingers.

Without warning, he makes like he's going to throw it at me.

Except it goes out, casting us into darkness. "Dammit!" he shouts.

I have no other choice. Picking up my hoop skirt, I break for the door.

30

We are always hiring new actors and actresses to work with our company. Preference given to those with great acting ability who can fold a fitted sheet and don't mind cleaning toilets.

I BARREL into the side of the doorframe, then out into the hallway. I race blindly down the hall, not knowing entirely where I am until I lunge into the table at the top of the staircase, sending whatever is atop it crashing to the floor. Changing direction, I rush toward the staircase, feeling for the railing. I stumble down a few steps before I grab onto the newel post, listening for him behind me.

The grandfather clock begins its Westminster chime. I take the stairs in a blind panic, nearly tumbling head over heels. *One…*

Between the chimes, his footfalls come behind me.

He knows this place so much better than I do. He is getting closer. *Two…*

"You can't escape." His voice is still calm. "There's nowhere to go, Sister."

Three…four…

I hit the bottom stair and lunge for the door, thinking I'll hide in the woods. As I'm working the lock, I remember the snow piled so high beyond the porch that Heath and I could barely move out more than a couple of feet. And that was over an hour ago.

Five…six…

I whirl around just as he reaches the bottom of the steps. I race across the foyer toward the dining room. I shove it with all my might.

It's locked.

Seven…eight…

I'm trapped.

"Are you ready for the end?"

Turning around, I face him. He comes up close to me, grisly mask and all, and I stiffen. The end is near. He'll light a match and throw it at me and burn Bug House to hell, where it belongs.

Nine…ten…

I wait. He seems unsure what to do, like he's waiting for *me* to act. I close my eyes. Finally, he says, "Are you ready, Sister?"

Yeah, he said that already. I hear the scrape of him trying to light another match. But nothing. Turns out, Sawyer is finding himself as useless with the old pack of matches as one of my kid siblings would be. It's a break of luck I hadn't anticipated. I let out a breath and open my eyes. My gaze falls on the doors to the Safe Room.

From this angle, I can clearly see a small sliver of light glowing underneath the door. A light I'm sure wasn't there earlier.

Pushing past him, I lunge for the door, astounded to find the mechanism in the handle releasing under my weight. It opens almost too readily, as if it had never been locked before. I shove open the doors and burst into a room of such blinding light that I'd have thought I went to heaven if I didn't already know this house was hell.

Before my eyes can adjust and the final chime can finish reverberating through my ears, another sound erupts, stunning me so that I fall backward.

31

Thank you for considering the Bismarck-Chisholm House
for your next event. We're dying to have you!

"SURPRISE!"

I blink. I blink again. My eyes are finally adjusting as I take
in the sight before me. My mother, dressed in a bright-red dress,
looks Boston chic, as if she never left. My siblings, bleary-eyed
but still excited, squirm with delight. Wit holds up the GoPro
to capture my astonished expression. Astrid stands next to him
in her ridiculous black wig. Although covered from chin to
chest in a dark strawberry stain, Becca still manages to rock that
red dress. Silly Sally is propped up on the leather sofa in her
flapper costume. And there are balloons. Lots of balloons. And
confetti. All the great makings of a party. On a table in front of
them sits a giant HAPPY BIRTHDAY, SEDA cake.

Zoe leans forward and dips her finger in the icing. "Are you
surprised, Seda? Are you? Are you?"

I whirl around to face Sawyer. The guy behind me lifts off his mask, grinning. It's Liam. "I thought for sure I was going to have to set you on fire before you noticed the light coming from this room."

My heart is still thumping from the danger. *This can't be happening.*

The kids rush to hug me as I let out a laugh that is part relief, part utter shock. Because nothing about what's happened tonight is funny. I look at my mom. "What...?"

She's smiling excitedly. "You said no one would buy this place. But you're wrong, Seda. We have a very interested buyer who wanted to see what we could do."

"What?"

Liam taps on his GoPro. "My dad. He's an investor. He was too busy to come up and check it out himself, but when he heard about this place, he was intrigued." He looks at my mom and holds up the camera. "I think this will seal the deal."

I look back toward the direction of the burned-out wing. "Sawyer..."

"Did we really have you believing that?" Mom laughs. "All that stuff was fake. I remember you being so convinced about your imaginary friend when you were a kid, so I thought it would make a great story line. Still, I was so nervous you'd figure it out it was a hoax. But I really believed in the idea, and some of my best theater students from last semester at BC decided to help me with it. The snowstorm coming along was just a bit of luck that made it extra exciting, don't you think?"

"I—" *It's all fake. Sawyer isn't real. He doesn't even exist, except...*

Just then, my stomach roils.

Adam grins at me and says, "Just for the record, I didn't really pee my pants."

I stare at him, his words echoing in my head. Every sound is distorted, battering my eardrums as Michael Jackson's "Thriller" plays in the background. My mother pats Adam's head and gives him a kiss. "My little actor."

I open my mouth to ask a question. I have a thousand whirling inside my head, and yet not one makes it out.

"I told you not to worry, Seda," my mom says, coming over and giving me a hug. "We're going to sell this place to Liam's father and get ourselves back to Boston for the spring semester. My sabbatical is over at the end of the year. And I bet you they'll want to use this story line for the hotel!"

We're going back to Boston. We're leaving Bug House. And new owners are going to put on a twisted act night after night, based on my life. As I stare at them all, smiling and hugging one another, I can hardly comprehend any of this. We're going back. Everything that happened tonight was just a game. Still, the roiling in my stomach becomes a thumping.

"You were right, Dr. H," Astrid says, thumping me on the back as if she's known me forever. She's wearing makeup on her face as if she's been burned. "Your daughter makes the perfect target! She had absolutely no clue. I do wish you'd have come in and seen my dead body though," she tells me. "It was *sweet*."

Wit is lounging on the leather sofa, snapping vampire fangs in and out of his mouth. "Yeah, but this was Heath's little drama. He gave us all character profiles and made us all study them so we could play our parts convincingly. Becca, the scaredy-cat. Liam, the loner. Me, the joker. Astrid, the tough girl. And Heath, the lothario."

"Wasn't much of a stretch for him," Becca quips, rolling her eyes, and the rest of them all chuckle knowingly.

Astrid nods. "It wasn't easy, pretending to be sweet sixteen again!"

"So what do you think, Dr. H?" Becca asks, nibbling on a tortilla chip. For the first time, she's not scared at all. She looks more relaxed and much prettier now, even with her hair all disheveled and the fake blood all over her face. She's in college. They all are. "You think Heath'll get an A on his senior thesis?"

I steady myself against the table. Heath. I think of him

and everything he'd said, how every one of his earnest words had tugged upon my heartstrings. That was by design. Sixteen, packed off to school at Shady View, destined to go to Stanford to become the Wiener King instead of pursuing his dreams, sad that his parents never had time for him.

It was all a lie.

Heath is a senior in college. And he's not going into business. He's an actor.

Everything he said, everything he did, was a lie. Choking on those brownies. Mourning his friends. Telling me he wanted to write to me. Giving me a *proper kiss*.

It was all an act. A fucking lie.

Right on cue, my stomach starts to burn, and it squeezes up into my throat.

"Where is the Wiener Prince of Pennsylvania, anyway?" Wit asks, spitting out the fangs and tossing a handful of popcorn into his mouth. He laughs. "That was a nice touch. He's the one who needs to celebrate the most. If it wasn't for those little details he threw in, improvising, Seda never would've fallen for it."

They all look around, everywhere but at me. Like I'm invisible. Like I'm the stupid one, the butt of this enormous joke. Of course, they don't see the one detail they should be noticing, a hole ripping their perfect little plan so wide apart that their lives will never be the same.

Because there's something they don't know: they won't hear him. Not until it's too late. That freezer door is far too thick.

I pat Heath's jacket pocket. Strange, I seem to have lost the key.

I'm hungry.

I know you are, I tell my brother in the voice only he can hear, patting my stomach gently. I slide into a chair and pull the largest piece of cake toward me. Sawyer needs to eat, and I need to do what he says. Because if I've learned anything from this experience, it's that I should listen to him more often.

After all, he knew something bad would happen. And he's always right.

ACKNOWLEDGMENTS

Thank you once again to Jennifer Murgia, for reading this book and helping me work out the kinks (and most importantly, the ending!). My sincerest gratitude goes out, as usual, to Mandy Hubbard, agent and friend from my very first book, who simply gets me as well as she gets the industry and understands the warped workings of my mind better than anyone I know. Also, big appreciation goes out to Annette Pollert-Morgan and the rest of the Sourcebooks team, for being so stellar to work with.

Love to my parents, who allowed me to watch slasher movies from a young age. Without you, and the twisted mind I got from those wonderfully sadistic movies, this book never would have been possible.

And of course, I can't heap enough praise, hugs, and kisses upon Brian, Sara, and Gabrielle, who remind me every day that real life isn't quite so scary. In fact, it's rather beautiful.

YOU THINK YOU KNOW WHAT HAPPENED.
YOU DON'T.

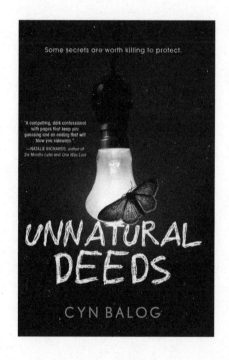

CHAPTER 1

Duchess—Police are investigating an apparent homicide after a body was found in a wooded area early Tuesday morning. Authorities have not yet released the name of the victim or the person(s) they are questioning in connection with the investigation.
—*Central Maine Express Times*

I<small>S THIS THING ON?</small>

Ha-ha, I'm a laugh a minute.

Anyway, Andrew. It's me. Vic. I wanted to say I'm sorry. Sorry for... Well, where do I begin? I—

Cough, cough, cough.

Sorry. I'm losing my voice. Something bitter is stuck in my throat, and the air is so cold it's hard to breathe. This place reeks of decaying leaves, of the musty, damp rot of dead things returning to the earth.

There's something soft and wet under my head. I hope it's not brain matter. I can't raise my arms to check because of the way I'm twisted here. I think my leg is broken. Or maybe my back? Damned if I can twitch a muscle without pain screaming its way up my spine.

Somehow I managed to pry my phone out of my jacket pocket and prop it on my chest, but you know how spotty service is around Duchess. All charged up with zero bars—not that I'd be calling anyone but you. I wish I could see the background photo of you and me. It'd keep me company. You know the one. It's the picture of us at the Renaissance Faire when we were fourteen. We're both grinning like mad and you have your arm around me, claiming me as your own. It's probably the only time you were ever comfortable with yourself. With us. I miss that.

Anyway, you know how glass half-empty I am, Andrew. I wanted to record a note for you on my phone. You know, in case I don't get out of here.

Of course I'll get out of here. I wouldn't be lucky enough to die here. But maybe this'll be easier than telling you in person.

Cough, cough.

Where should I start?

It's so quiet. You must have left me, Andrew. But

you'll come back. You always come back. You were scared, maybe, when you saw what you'd done. And now I'm all alone here.

I don't really know where "here" is. I think it's a drainage ditch on the side of Route 11. The last thing I remember is rushing down the road near the Kissing Woods, feeling powerful. Immortal. Like everything I wanted could be mine. For an instant, I felt like *he* could be mine.

But that's not possible now.

I know what people have said behind my back in hushed whispers. They call me delusional. But I'm not. I know what is real and what isn't.

No, wait. The last thing I remember is you with that fierce look in your eyes. You sure surprised me. Who knew that my boyfriend, quiet, unassuming Andrew Quinn, had *that* in him?

I thought I knew you inside and out, but…I was wrong.

I guess I should explain. After all, I have no other pressing engagements. And you're overdue an explanation, aren't you? The tall pines can be my witnesses. They can pass judgment as they see fit.

I'm not sure when it all began, but Lady M said it best. Hell is goddamn murky.

Whoops. Blasphemy. Yet another sin to add to my act-of-contrition list.

Looking back, you knew when I started to change, didn't you, Andrew? You know everything about me. It was that very first day of school, the day my life began and the day it began to unravel.

So here are the gory details. It won't be enough, but I'll try. You can't know it all until you've smelled that intoxicating cinnamon-and-cloves scent, read those texts that elevated even the blandest words to poetry, and seen those heart-stoppingly blue eyes.

His eyes. Even now, I can see them with perfect clarity. I've seen them in my dreams, in the sky when the sun hits the clouds just right, and in my morning breakfast cereal. It all goes back to him. Every single thought always winds *right back to him. Always. Always. Always.*

It's no use. I want him out of my head. I wish I could scrape him out of my memory. I don't want to live with him etched in the deepest part of me. I don't want to die thinking of him.

But I know I will.

CHAPTER 2

Abigail Zell of 12 Spruce Street called at 8:33 a.m. to report her daughter's disappearance. The girl, Victoria Zell, 16, a student at St. Ann's Catholic School in Bangor, was not in her bed when her mother went to wake her for school. Officer advised Mrs. Zell that missing persons report can be filed after a 24-hour waiting period.

—*Duchess Police Department phone log*

DO YOU REMEMBER THAT NIGHT, Andrew? Right before I started junior year? We were crouched in our hiding place, between the rosebushes at the white picket fence separating our yards, you on your side, me on mine. Just like bookends. The grass stopped growing where I used to plant my backside, but it was thick on your side, probably the result of your mom's green thumb. It was already chilly, the crickets chirruping their summer goodbye. When I was young, I used to count fireflies while we talked. That night, there were no fireflies.

"Vic," you whispered through the fence.

I giggled, lovesick. I adore your voice. It's so low and musical, even when you're not singing. If a voice made a whole person, I would be utterly, desperately in love with you. Most of the time, it's painful to watch you struggle to get the words out. Not because it bothers me, but because I know how much it bothers *you*. You've never liked yourself much, but I think you hate your wayward tongue most of all. How can something that behaves so angelically while singing music betray you so terribly the rest of the time?

You rarely stutter with me. When we were alone and darkness cloaked us, your voice was perfect. *Life* was perfect then. Stupidly, I didn't realize it.

"Y-you have fun at school tomorrow, OK?"

"Fun?"

You paused. "OK. Don't run screaming from school tomorrow. Better?"

"Much." I pushed a piece of foil-wrapped Juicy Fruit between the slats. A second later, I could hear you chewing the gum. "I wish you would be there."

I felt you push against the fence. You liked to fold the silver paper into squares and wedge them between the slats. "Save your wishes," you muttered.

It's true that wishing was useless. As if your mother would suddenly decide not to homeschool you so you could enroll at St. Ann's. As if you'd be able to enter a classroom without crumpling into a panicky mess.

"You out there still?" Your stepfather's voice boomed from the darkness.

I peered between the slats at the lit tip of his cigarette, cutting through the darkness near your back porch. Since he worked so much of the time, all I ever saw of your stepdad was that tiny orange fireball. You jumped to attention and the fence rattled. "Y-y-y-yes, sir," you said.

I poked my head up and your stepdad muttered something about me. Nothing nice, I'm sure. Your stepdad has never been the sweetest of men, which makes him the opposite of your mom. You told me the story about a thousand times, about how they married when you were seven, mostly because your dad died unexpectedly and left you two in major debt… A "marriage of convenience" you'd said, but it never seemed very convenient for you. Your mother is prim and proper and likes the finer things in life, and your stepfather, well, doesn't. Somehow though, they fit together. There's only one piece in that puzzle that never seemed to fit. You.

I told you good night, then turned to go inside. My parents had the kitchen blinds parted in a vee, squinting into the dark yard in their attempt to spy on us. "Good night, Vic," you called to me. Most people call me Victoria. People are always formal with me. They think I am oh-so-serious and uptight because I don't know them well enough to say, "Hey, let's not be formal. Vic's fine." And, well, I can't help it. "Relax" is a mantra I repeat over and over in my head. And do I ever? Nope.

Victoria is a serious name, an old name. Everything about me screams old, from the way I dress to my often-hunched posture. Even my hands look old, veined and thin and fragile.

I guess we're just two peas in a pod, Andrew: You and your premature balding, and me and my old-lady habits. You and your agoraphobia, and me and my crippling anxiety. We belong together. And yet something in me wanted more. I am sorry to say that I wanted what I knew couldn't be. What *shouldn't* be.

And because of that, I blindly let him lead me.

CHAPTER 3

When did you realize something was off?

Off... What do you mean?

When did things start to change? Can you pinpoint when the trouble began?

Oh. It had to be that very first day he walked into the classroom. He...he infused the room with... It's hard to explain. Energy, I guess?

In a good way?

Well, yeah. Mostly. He spurred people into action, made things happen. But...I guess not all of that was good.

—*Police interview with Rachel Watson, junior at St. Ann's*

I KNOW YOU CAN'T FORGIVE ME, Andrew. I fastened the collar around my own neck and handed him the leash.

But some people—oh, some people are just so damn like that. Intoxicating. Spellbinding. You find yourself aching to belong to them, dreading freedom, thinking freedom itself is the cage.

My mom had my lunch packed and ready. She had all my pencils sharpened and supplies organized in my L. L. Bean backpack. Breakfast was lined up for me on the counter: a banana, a glass of OJ, one Effexor, and an Ativan. The Effexor was usually all I needed to control my anxiety. I only took the Ativan for super-stressful situations, and I guess my mom assumed this qualified. As I sucked down the pills, she asked me how I was doing and if I was ready for the three-thousandth time.

I swear my parents barely let me breathe on my own anymore.

Honestly, I didn't feel nervous at all. I knew the Ativan would combat any first-day-back freak-outs; it usually works like a charm.

Usually.

I felt magically good for an entire hour. Believe it or not, that morning, as I waited for the bus to school, I thought only of you. And I smiled. You've always been my constant, easily readable, black and white, like the piano keys you adore. The first day of my junior year was sure to be more of me hiding behind my books, then rushing home to complain to you, just as I'd done during my first year at St. Ann's. You always listened, no matter how much I ranted. Back then, that patch of dirt in the backyard was my haven, my sanctuary... Like you, I wanted nothing more than constancy.

The bus ride into Bangor was mostly uneventful, long as it was. Most kids in the upper grades drove or carpooled together, so I was stuck with a handful of chatty, jumper-wearing elementary-school girls. I didn't mind. I looked out the window and watched the tall pines of rural Maine as we passed.

The real nerves didn't hit me until after I sat down at my desk.

That's when I met him.

That morning I had on my uniform from last year. My old, pilled plaid skirt that I'd bought two sizes too big with hopes of scraping through senior year before it was above my knees. My Peter Pan–collared blouse was wrinkled, but it is butt-ugly even when it's nicely pressed. My knee-highs had long since lost their elasticity and had already begun to descend toward my scuffed loafers, but the right one was winning by several inches. I never cut my hair, so a ponytail was the best style my stick-straight, beige hair could manage. Activities my classmates lived for—shopping, getting a car, partying—hardly mattered to me. Little did I know, that was about to change.

When I got to my homeroom, number 46B, the junior room, all the desks were arranged in rows of five, as usual. The symmetry hit me right away. There were only twenty-nine kids in my class: fifteen girls and fourteen boys. I knew this well because last year, they'd pair up for projects and lab experiments, leaving me out in Siberia.

But now, there were thirty desks.

I hurried to my seat in the back corner. My last name always lands me at the end of everything. I put my brown-bag lunch on the desk and waited for the other students to arrive. They filtered in, sporting summer tans and crisp, new school uniforms. None of them looked at me. I was OK with that. I figured it went with the territory of being the New Kid in a class where all the other students had known each other since kindergarten.

When Z arrived, everyone stared. His body seemed to absorb the attention. He stood straighter, glowed more. Z sauntered, hands in his pockets, looking straight ahead, like nobody else existed. He didn't carry anything, as if lugging books or a bag or whatever was beneath him. He just had a pencil behind his ear, drowning in his unruly, golden mop of hair. He was tan and had nice stubble on his chin, like a full-grown man. But it was those eyes. Like a baby's eyes, they took up half his face. They made me think of billiards, even though I only watched you play, Andrew. His eyes were bluer than pool cue chalk.

In a split second I went from New Kid to…nobody.

I peeked at him for only a second. A guy like that wouldn't notice me, wouldn't even say "excuse me" if he smacked me on the head with, say, a pool cue. I watched everyone else gawk. Parker Cole ran her perfect tongue over her glossy lips and threw doe eyes his way. Her arsenal of sweet, sexy looks was as abundant as her collection of fuzzy black sweaters. She was wearing one over her uniform, which I'm sure was not regulation, but having a dad as principal has its advantages.

Even though Principal Cole's morning announcements always included a plug for going green, Parker never rode in with him. No, he had an SUV, and she commuted in from the coast in a bright-red sports car that could stop traffic from all the way over the New Hampshire state line. I'd never seen the Cole family estate, but I imagined it to be majestic and storybook perfect, with breathtaking ocean views.

I realized everyone was looking at me. Me,

nothing-to-see-here, back-corner-hugging Victoria Zell. But that was because *he* was standing over me.

"I believe you're in my seat," he said.

His voice resounded like yours, Andrew, so like the voice that constantly lulls me out of my bad moods and comforts me during the worst days.

I almost looked around for you, but I shrugged, then pulled out my brand-new notebook. "Er. No. I always sit here."

"Alphabetical?" he asked.

"Yes. I'm Zell."

He thrust his hand under my nose.

"Zachary Zimmerman. People call me Z. Nice to meet you."

DON'T MISS UNNATURAL DEEDS— AND THE ELECTRIFYING ENDING YOU WON'T SEE COMING...

ABOUT THE AUTHOR

Cyn Balog is the author of a number of young adult novels. She lives outside Allentown, Pennsylvania, with her husband and daughters. Visit her online at cynbalog.com.

BEA T BAL

Are you
FIRED UP about YA?
Don't Miss the HOT New YA Newsletter
from Sourcebooks Fire

 FIREreads

⑤ #GetBookLit

FEATURING:
Author interviews
Galley giveaways
Exclusive early content
What's new each month
...and more!

Visit books.sourcebooks.com/firereads-ya to sign up!

Follow the FIREreads team and share your
burning love for YA with #GetBookLit:

 @sourcebooksfire   sourcebooksfire

 SourcebooksFire   firereads.tumblr.com

 sourcebooks
fire